Petersburg Tales

Nikolai Gogol

Translated by Dora O'Brien

ALMA CLASSICS

ALMA CLASSICS LTD
London House
243-253 Lower Mortlake Road
Richmond
Surrey TW9 2LL
United Kingdom
www.almaclassics.com

The four stories in this collection first published in Russian in 1834–42.
This edition first published by Alma Books Ltd in 2014

Translation © Dora O'Brien, 2014

Cover image © nathanburtondesign.com

Printed and bound by CPI Group (UK) Ltd, Croydon, CR0 4YY

ISBN: 978-1-84749-349-1

All rights reserved. No part of this publication may be reproduced, stored in or introduced into a retrieval system, or transmitted, in any form or by any means (electronic, mechanical, photocopying, recording or otherwise), without the prior written permission of the publisher. This book is sold subject to the condition that it shall not be resold, lent, hired out or otherwise circulated without the express prior consent of the publisher.

Contents

Petersburg Tales   1

   Nevsky Prospect   3

   The Nose   56

   The Overcoat   95

   Diary of a Madman   143

   Note on the Text   177

   Notes   177

Petersburg Tales

Nevsky Prospect

THERE IS NOTHING TO COMPARE with Nevsky Prospect,* at least not in St Petersburg, where it embodies everything. There is no end to the glamour of this street – the belle of our capital city! I know that not one of its pale and high-ranking residents would exchange Nevsky Prospect for the world. Not only the twenty-five-year-old who sports a splendid moustache and a remarkably well-tailored frock coat, but even the individual with white bristles sprouting from his chin and a head as smooth as a silver dish, even he is ecstatic about Nevsky Prospect. As for the ladies! Oh, Nevsky Prospect is even more of a delight to the ladies. Indeed, is there anyone it doesn't delight? The moment you step onto Nevsky Prospect there is an air of pure conviviality. You may be on some vital, pressing errand, but you will most likely forget all about it once you have taken that step. This is the only place where people come neither out of necessity nor driven by their own compulsion or those business interests that consume the whole of St Petersburg. It is as though a person you meet on Nevsky Prospect is less selfish than on Morskaya, Gorokhovaya, Liteynaya, Meshchanskaya or on other streets where greed

3

and profit and compulsion are manifest both in those on foot and those flying past in their carriages and droshkies. Nevsky Prospect is the communication hub of St Petersburg. Here a resident of the Petersburg or Vyborg districts who, for several years, has not been to see his friend at Peski or the Moscow Gate* can be sure to bump into him. No directory or enquiry desk will deliver such reliable information as Nevsky Prospect. Almighty Nevsky Prospect! The only place in St Petersburg where a poor man can enjoy himself! How neatly its pavements are swept and, God, how many feet have left their mark on it. The lumbering muddy boot of the former soldier, under whose weight the granite itself seems to crack, and the minuscule slipper, light as a wisp of smoke, of the young lady who has turned her little head towards the shining shop windows like a sunflower turns to the sun, and the clanking sabre of the hopeful ensign as it sharply scratches its surface – all unleash upon it either the force of strength or the force of weakness. What a rapid phantasmagoria takes place on it within a single day! How many changes it endures in just twenty-four hours!

Let's start in the very early morning, when the whole of St Petersburg smells of hot freshly baked loaves and is filled with old women in tattered dresses and coats besieging churches and charitable passers-by. At that time Nevsky Prospect is deserted: stocky shopkeepers and their assistants are still asleep in their cotton nightshirts or else lathering their fine

4

cheeks and drinking coffee. The destitute gather by the doors of patisseries, where a sleepy Ganymede,* who the day before had been flitting like a fly carrying chocolate drinks, now crawls out, broom in hand, tieless, and tosses stale pies and leftovers to them. Workers trudge along the streets; now and then Russian muzhiks cross over it as they hurry to work in their lime-stained boots which even the waters of the Catherine Canal,* noted for its purity, would be unable to wash off. At that time of day it is usually unseemly for ladies to be out and about, because Russian folk like to use strong language such as they would probably never hear even in the theatre. Occasionally a sleepy clerk drags himself along with a briefcase under his arm if Nevsky Prospect happens to be on his way to the office. One can definitely say that at this time, until twelve o'clock that is, Nevsky Prospect is no one's objective: it is used purely as an expedient. It gradually fills up with individuals with their own pursuits, worries and disappointments, but who do not spare it a thought. The Russian muzhik talks about the *grivna** or penny coppers, old men and women gesticulate or talk to themselves, sometimes accompanied by rather bizarre gestures, but nobody listens to them or laughs at them save perhaps street urchins in coarse striped smocks carrying empty bottles or newly repaired boots as they race along Nevsky Prospect at lightning speed. At this time of day, however you are dressed, even if you are wearing a peaked cap rather than a hat, or if your collar sticks out too much above your tie, no one will notice.

At twelve o'clock Nevsky Prospect is overrun by tutors of all nationalities with their pupils in batiste collars. English Joneses and French Coqs walk arm in arm with the charges entrusted to their parental care and, with suitable aplomb, they explain to them that the signs above the shops are put there to allow us to discover what is to be found inside those shops. Governesses, pale misses and rosy-cheeked Slavs step majestically behind their dainty fidgety little girls, telling them to lift up their shoulders and straighten their backs; in short, at this time Nevsky Prospect is a pedagogical Nevsky Prospect. But the closer it gets to two o'clock, the more the number of tutors, teachers and children dwindles; in the end they are supplanted by their fond fathers strolling arm in arm with their flashy, brightly arrayed, weak-nerved companions. They are gradually joined by all those who have completed their fairly important domestic tasks, such as discussing the weather and the sudden appearance of a small pimple on the nose with their doctor, enquiring about the health of their horses and children – who by the way show great promise – or reading a poster and an important newspaper article about the comings and goings of people, and finally having a cup of coffee or tea; and they in turn are joined by those whom an enviable fate has endowed with the blessed title of officials with special responsibilities.*

They are joined in turn by those who serve in the Foreign Office and are distinguished by the nobility of their pursuits and their habits. God, what wonderful posts and jobs there are! How they animate and delight the soul! But alas! I'm not a civil servant and I'm denied the pleasure of witnessing how delicately my superiors treat me. Everything you come across on Nevsky Prospect is imbued with propriety: men in long frock coats, hands in pockets, ladies in pink, white and pale-blue satin redingotes and hats. Here you will encounter unique side whiskers, tucked under the necktie with unusual and amazing skill, velvety side whiskers, satiny ones, side whiskers as black as sable or coal – but those alas belong solely to the Foreign Office. Providence has prohibited black side whiskers for those who serve in other departments: they must, to their great chagrin, wear ginger ones. Here you will encounter marvellous moustaches that no pen or brush could depict, moustaches to whom the better part of a lifetime has been devoted – objects of long vigils, night and day – moustaches which have been sprayed with the most delightful perfumes and aromas and pomaded with the most precious and rare assortments of creams, moustaches twisted by night in thin vellum paper, moustaches on which their owners bestow the most touching devotion and which are the envy of all passers-by. Thousands of varieties of hats, dresses, scarves – colourful and dainty – which hold the affection of their wearers for sometimes two whole days will bedazzle just about anyone on Nevsky Prospect. It is as though an entire sea of butterflies has suddenly surged up from flower stalks, forming a bright cloud rippling above black beetles of the male sex. Here you will encounter such waists as you have never even dreamt of: so slender and slight, no thicker than a bottle's neck; waists which, when chanced upon, you will respectfully dodge to avoid inadvertently jostling them with a rude elbow: your heart is overcome by bashfulness and fear lest even a reckless breath of yours could snap this most charm-ing work of nature and art in two. And what ladies' sleeves you will encounter on Nevsky Prospect! Oh, what a delight! They bear some resemblance to two hot-air balloons, so that a lady might suddenly be lifted up into the air were there not a man to hold on to her; for it is as pleasant and as easy to lift a lady up into the air as raise a champagne-filled glass to one's lips. Nowhere do people exchange bows so magnanimously and freely upon meeting each other as they do on Nevsky Prospect. This is where you will encounter a unique smile, a smile that transcends art, a smile that at times makes you melt with pleasure, at times makes you bow your head down as you see yourself all of a sudden lower than the grass or makes you lift it up as you feel yourself soaring above Admiralty Spire.* Here you will meet people conversing about a concert or the weather with singular grandeur and self-esteem. Here you will encounter thousands of inscrutable characters and phenomena.

O Creator! What extraordinary characters one comes across on Nevsky Prospect! There are many such people who, when meeting you, invariably look at your shoes, and if you have walked past, they will turn round to look at your coat tails. I've yet to understand why this is. At first I imagined they were shoemakers, but that, however, was certainly not the case: they mostly serve in various departments, and many of them are perfectly able to write a memorandum from one government department to another; or else they are people who spend their time going out, reading newspapers in patisseries – in other words, most of them are respectable people. This hallowed hour between two and three in the afternoon, which could be known as Nevsky Prospect at its most bustling, is when the main exhibition of man's best endeavours takes place. One sports a dandified frock coat with the best beaver fur, another a remarkable Greek nose, a third has superb side whiskers, a fourth has beautiful eyes and a striking hat, a fifth wears a talisman ring on his dainty little finger, a sixth flaunts her little foot in a charming little shoe, a seventh wears a tie that provokes astonishment, an eighth a moustache that knocks you down with amazement. But the clock strikes three and the exhibition is over, the crowd thins out… At three o'clock there is another change of scene. Spring has suddenly arrived on Nevsky Prospect: it is swamped entirely by civil servants in green uniforms. Hungry titular councillors, court councillors and the rest all do their very best to quicken their step. Young collegiate registrars, provincial and collegiate secretaries hurry to make the most of their time and walk along Nevsky Prospect with a demeanour that belies the fact that they have just sat in their office for six hours. But the older collegiate secretaries and titular and court councillors walk briskly with their heads bowed: they have no business scrutinizing passers-by: they have not quite torn themselves away from their concerns. Their heads are still full of clutter and whole archives of unfinished matters; for a long time, instead of shop signs, they see a box of documents or the Office Director's round face.

Nevsky Prospect remains deserted from four o'clock on, and it is doubtful you will come across a single clerk. The odd seamstress from a shop might run across Nevsky Prospect holding a box, or else the pitiful victim of a philanthropic lawyer, with only a fleecy overcoat to call his own; or some visiting eccentric who takes no notice of the hour; or a tall thin Englishwoman carrying a handbag and a book; or a workman, a Russian in a thick cotton frock coat gathered at the back, with a wispy little beard, who spends his life just anyhow, and forever twitches his back and arms and legs and head as he steps circumspectly along the pavement; or occasionally some humble artisan. You will meet no one else on Nevsky Prospect.

But as soon as dusk descends upon the houses and streets and the duty policeman, having covered himself with matting, clambers up a ladder to light the street lamp, and those prints that dare not expose themselves in daylight now appear in small ground-level shop windows, then Nevsky Prospect revives and begins to stir. Then comes that mysterious time of day when street lamps give everything an enticing, wonderful glow. You will encounter very many young men, mostly bachelors, in warm frock coats and overcoats. At this time there is a feeling of purpose, or rather something akin to purpose, something utterly baffling; everyone's pace quickens and generally becomes very uneven. Long shadows flash along walls and pavement, their heads very nearly reaching Police Bridge. Young collegiate registrars and provincial and collegiate secretaries spend a very long time strolling up and down the street, but the elderly collegiate registrars and titular and court councillors mostly stay at home, either because they are married or because their live-in German cooks prepare delicious meals for them. Here you will encounter those esteemed old men who at two o'clock strolled with such self-importance and amazing dignity along Nevsky Prospect. You will see them running along like young collegiate registrars to take a peep under the hat of some lady spotted from afar, whose fleshy lips and heavily rouge-plastered cheeks are so pleasing to many of those who walk by, but above all to those tradesmen, workmen and merchants who always wear German frock coats and walk about in large groups, usually arm in arm.

"Stop!" Lieutenant Pirogov called out at that time of day, tugging at a young man in cloak and tails who was walking beside him. "Did you see that?"

"I did. She's amazing, truly Perugino's Bianca."*

"Who are you talking about?"

"That one, the one with dark hair. And what eyes! My God, what eyes! Her whole bearing and figure and her profile – it's a wonder!"

"I'm talking about the blonde who was behind her over there. Why don't you go after the brunette if you like her that much?"

"How can I?" exclaimed the young man in tails, blushing. "As if she were one of those who stroll along Nevsky Prospect in the evenings; she must be a very distinguished lady," he continued with a sigh. "Her cloak alone is worth around eighty roubles."

"You fool!" cried out Pirogov, pushing him hard towards where her bright cloak was fluttering. "Go on, you ninny, you'll miss your chance! I'll go after the blonde."

The two friends went their separate ways.

"We know what you're all like," mused Pirogov with a self-satisfied confident smile, convinced that no beauty could resist him.

The young man in cloak and tails stepped timidly and anxiously towards where the colourful cloak was fluttering in the distance, now flashing brightly as it approached a street lamp, now momentarily covered in darkness as it moved away from it. His heart was pounding, and he instinctively quickened his step. He dared not even think of having any claim on the attention of that beauty who was flying off in the distance, let alone allowing himself any of the lewd thoughts that Lieutenant Pirogov had hinted at. All he wanted was to see the house, catch sight of the dwelling place of that heavenly creature who seemed to have flown down from heaven straight onto Nevsky Prospect and who would most likely fly off God knows where. He rushed ahead so fast that he repeatedly knocked sedate grey-whiskered gentlemen off the pavement. This young man belonged to a class of people which constitutes quite a strange phenomenon among us, and he belongs as much to the citizens of St Petersburg as a person who appears in our dreams does to the real world. This exceptional social group is very uncommon in this city, where everyone is either a civil servant, a merchant or a German craftsman. He was an artist. Is that not indeed a strange phenomenon? A St Petersburg artist! An artist in the land of snow, an artist in the land of the Finns, where all is wet, plain, level, pale, grey and misty. These artists have nothing in common with Italian artists – proud, passionate like Italy itself and its sky – on the contrary, these are mostly kind, meek folk, timid, easy-going, quietly enjoying their art, drinking tea with a couple of friends in small rooms, modestly discussing their favourite topic and showing no interest at all in anything else. They are always inviting some old beggar woman to their place, making her sit for a good six hours in order to commit her pathetic impassive countenance to canvas. They paint a perspective of their room, which is full of artistic junk: plaster casts of arms and legs turned coffee-coloured with time and dust, broken easels, an overturned palette, a guitar-playing friend, walls daubed in paint, an open window through which you glimpse the pale River Neva and poor fishermen in red shirts. They almost all use greyish dull colours – the indelible hallmark of the north. They do however apply themselves to their task with genuine pleasure. They often foster real talent within themselves, and if only Italy's fresh air were to blow on them, this talent would flourish as freely, widely and brightly as a plant that is finally brought out of a room into the open air. They are on the whole very self-effacing: a star and a thick epaulette throw them into such confusion that they automatically lower the price of their artwork. They occasionally enjoy playing the dandy a little, but this dandyism always comes across as too drastic and a bit random. You might at times come across them in an excellent tailcoat and a grubby cloak, or an expensive velvet waistcoat and a frock coat smeared with paint. Similarly, on one of their unfinished landscapes you will sometimes see a nymph's head, painted at the bottom of the canvas, which the artist, for lack of space, had sketched on the soiled backdrop of a previous painting he had once worked on with delight. They never look you straight in the eye; if they do, it will be a somewhat dull and vague look: they do not pierce you with the hawk-like gaze of an observer or the falcon-like stare of a cavalry officer. This is because, as they register your features, they will simultaneously see those of some plaster cast of Hercules that stands in their room or have in mind a picture they still want to paint. That is why they often reply incoherently, sometimes inappropriately, and the muddle in their heads only magnifies their bashfulness. To this class belonged the young man we have described, the artist Piskarev, diffident and shy, but harbouring in his soul sparks of feeling ready, given the right opportunity, to burst into flame. He hurried with secret trepidation in pursuit of the object that had so affected him, and he seemed taken aback by his own boldness. The unknown creature to whom his eyes, thoughts and feelings were so drawn suddenly turned her head and glanced at him. God, what divine features! The most charming dazzlingly white brow was fringed by hair as beautiful as agate. These magnificent locks, some showing below her hat, cascaded in curls and brushed a cheek delicately flushed by the evening chill. Her lips held on tightly to a host of utterly delightful daydreams. All that is left from childhood memories or that brings on dreams and quiet inspiration by the light of a lamp – all that seemed to blend, merge and be reflected in her perfectly shaped lips. She glanced at Piskarev, and his heart quivered at her look. She looked at him sternly, her face showing a sense of indignation at such an impertinent pursuit; but even anger looked bewitching on that beautiful face. Overcome with shame and shyness, he stopped, lowering his glance; but how could he lose sight of that divine being and not even discover the sacred place where she dwelt? Those were the thoughts that crossed the young dreamer's mind, and he resolved to pursue her. But to avoid being noticed he hung back, looking around casually, examining shop signs but all the while not losing sight of a single step taken by the unknown girl. Passers-by had begun to flit by less frequently, the street grew quieter; the beauty glanced back, and it seemed to him that the hint of a smile flickered on her lips. He shivered and could not believe his eyes. No, it was that street lamp with its deceptive beam that had projected the semblance of a smile on her face – no, his own daydreams were mocking him. His breath faltered in his breast: he was overcome by an indefinable trembling fit; his senses were on fire and everything in front of him was turning misty. The pavement fled under him, carriages with their galloping horses appeared motionless, the bridge was expanding and splitting at the arch, a house stood on its roof, the sentry box was collapsing towards him, and the sentry's halberd, along with the golden lettering and the painted scissors of a shop sign, seemed to glow on his very eyelash. And a single glance, a single turn of a pretty head had generated all this. Not hearing or seeing or taking in anything, he rushed after the light footsteps of those beautiful little feet, trying to temper the speed of his own steps as they flew in time with his heartbeat. Sometimes he was overcome by doubt as to whether her expression had really been so friendly – and he would stop for an instant, but his pounding heart and the irresistible force and turmoil of his feelings urged him onwards. He did not even notice how a four-storey house rose before him, how four rows of lit-up windows suddenly stared at him and how the railing by the entrance confronted him with its iron impact. He saw the stranger fly up the stairs, look back, lay a finger to her lips and make a sign to follow her. His knees trembled; his senses and thoughts were on fire; a lightning bolt of joy pierced his heart with unbearable keenness. No, this was no dream! God, so much happiness in a split second! Such a wonderful life in just a couple of minutes!

But was he not asleep and dreaming all this? Could it be that she, for whose single heavenly glance he was ready to give up his life, the approach to whose dwelling place he regarded already as indescribable bliss, could it be that she had really been so well disposed and attentive towards him just now? He flew up the stairs. His thoughts were not of the earthly kind, nor was he inflamed by earthly passion – no, in that instant he was pure and chaste, like a virgin youth still breathing an indefinable spiritual need for love. And that which would have aroused brazen thoughts in a depraved individual made his, on the contrary, all the purer. This trust shown him by a frail, beautiful creature, this trust imposed on him a vow of chivalrous rigor, a vow of slavishly fulfilling her every command. He only wished those commands to be as arduous and hard to fulfil as possible, so that he could then fly to overcome them with the greatest exertion. He had no doubt that some secret and at the same time momentous event had forced the unknown girl to place herself in his hands, that considerable service would surely be required of him, and he already felt he had the strength and determination for anything.

The flight of stairs went spiralling upwards, and with them spiralled his fast-paced dreams. "Watch how you go!" rang out a harp-like voice, filling him to the core with renewed trepidation. In the dark heights of the fourth floor the unknown girl knocked on a door: it opened and they both went in. A rather good-looking woman holding a candle met them, but she stared at Piskarev in such a queer and insolent manner that he instinctively lowered his eyes. They entered a room. Three female figures in different corners appeared before his eyes. One was laying out cards, another sat at a piano playing some sad imitation of an old polonaise with two fingers, a third one sat in front of a mirror, combing her long hair without feeling the need to abandon her toilette at the arrival of a stranger. A sort of unpleasant clutter, the kind you only find in a bachelor's neglected room, ruled everywhere. Rather nice furniture was covered in dust, a spider had spun its web over the moulded cornice, and through the open door to another room a spurred boot shone and the edging of a uniform flashed red; a man's loud voice and female laughter resounded without any restraint.

God, where had he landed! He did not want to believe it at first, and began to peer at the objects in the room more intently, but the bare walls and the curtainless windows did not point to the presence of a conscientious housewife; the jaded faces of those pitiful creatures, one of whom sat almost right by his nose and was examining him as calmly as she would a stain on someone's dress, all this convinced him that he had entered one of those despicable dens where wretched depravity – produced by the capital's tawdry cultural standards and appalling overcrowding – had established its base. A den where man irreverently crushed and mocked everything pure and holy that enhanced life; where woman, this beauty of our world, the pinnacle of creation, turned into a bizarre ambiguous being; where, along with her pure soul she forfeited everything feminine and distastefully adopted the manner and impudence of men and so ceased to be that frail beautiful creature, so distinct from us. Piskarev sized her up and down with bewildered eyes, as though wanting to make sure that she was the one who had so bewitched him and swept him away on Nevsky Prospect. Yet there she stood in front of him, just as lovely as before: her hair was just as beautiful, her eyes still seemed divine. She was fresh; she was only seventeen, and it was apparent that terrible depravity had only recently caught up with her. It had not yet dared touch her cheeks: they were fresh and lightly tinged with a delicate flush – she was magnificent.

He stood unmoving before her and was ready to lose himself as simple-heartedly as he had done before. But the beautiful girl became bored with such a lengthy silence and gave a meaningful smile, looking him straight in the eye. Yet that smile was filled with a kind of abject insolence: it was such an odd smile and was as much in tune with her face as a pious expression is with a bribe-taker's ugly mug or a bookkeeper's ledger is with a poet. He shuddered. She parted her gorgeous lips and began to say something, but it was all so stupid, so vulgar… as though a person's mind leaves him when he loses his chastity. He no longer wanted to hear anything. He was utterly ridiculous and naive, like a child. Instead of taking advantage of such favours, instead of rejoicing at such a situation, which no doubt anyone else in his place would have done, he took to his heels like a wild goat and ran out onto the street.

With his head hung low and his arms limp, he sat in his room like a wretch who had found a priceless pearl and had there and then dropped it into the sea. "Such a beauty, such divine features – and where is she? In that kind of a place!…" That was all he was able to utter.

We're indeed never more seized by pity than when we see beauty touched by the putrid breath of depravity. Let ugliness befriend it, but beauty, tender beauty... in our minds it can only be combined with chastity and purity. The beauty who had so bewitched poor Piskarev was indeed a wonderful, extraordinary apparition. Her presence in that sordid milieu seemed even more extraordinary. Each feature of hers was so purely formed, the expression on her lovely face implied such nobility, that it was impossible to believe that depravity had sunk its horrific claws into her. She could have been the priceless pearl, the whole world, the whole of paradise, the entire wealth of a passionate husband. She could have been a beautiful silent star in an ordinary family circle, issuing her sweet commands with one movement of her lovely lips. She could have been a divine being in a crowded ballroom, on a bright parquet floor, by candlelight, with the speechless awe of a crowd of admirers prostrate at her feet. But alas! By some horrifying fancy of a hellish spirit that craved to destroy life's harmony, she had been flung with a cackle into its abyss.

He sat by the low-burning candle filled with agonizing sadness. It was already long past midnight: the tower clock struck half-past twelve and he sat motionless, neither sleeping nor properly awake. Drowsiness, taking advantage of his stillness, was about to overpower him by stealth; the room was already beginning to fade away: only the single candle flame shone through the dreams overwhelming him, when a sudden knock on the door made him start and come to his senses. The door opened and a footman in a rich livery walked in. No rich livery had ever made an appearance before in his solitary room, especially at such an unusual hour… He was dumbfounded and looked at the footman with impatient curiosity.

"The lady," the footman pronounced with a courteous bow, "whose house you were pleased to visit a few hours ago, has bid me invite you to come to her and sent her carriage for you."

Piskarev stood speechless with astonishment. "A carriage, a footman in livery! No, there must surely be some mistake…"

"Listen here, my good man," he said timidly. "You probably didn't mean to come here. Your mistress undoubtedly sent for someone else, not me."

"No, sir, I've not made a mistake. It was you, was it not, who accompanied the lady on foot to her house on Liteynaya Street, up to a room on the fourth floor?"

"Yes, it was."

"Well then, please do hurry. My lady wishes to see you without fail and invites you to go straight to her house."

Piskarev rushed down the stairs. A carriage was indeed standing outside. He took a seat, the doors slammed, the cobblestones rumbled beneath the wheels and hooves, and the illuminated prospect of buildings with bright signboards flashed by the carriage windows. Piskarev remained deep in thought throughout the journey and was unable to explain this adventure. Her own house, a carriage, a footman in rich livery... he could not reconcile this in any way with the room on the fourth floor, the dusty windows and the out-of-tune piano.

The carriage came to a halt in front of a brightly lit entrance, and he was struck at once by the row of carriages, the chatter of coachmen, the brightly lit windows and the sounds of music. The richly liveried footman helped him out of the carriage and respectfully led him into a foyer with marble columns, a doorman dripping in gold, a scattering of cloaks and furs and a glowing lamp. A light, sweetly scented stairway with shiny banisters flew upwards. He was already on the stairs, had already entered the first hall, struck with terror and shying away at the first step from the ghastly crush of people. The extraordinary medley of faces threw him into a state of total confusion: it seemed to him that some demon had chopped the whole world into lots of different pieces and had mixed all those pieces up without rhyme or reason. Ladies' gleaming shoulders and black tailcoats, chandeliers, lamps, vaporous fluttering gauzes, wispy ribbons and a stout double bass emerging from behind the railings of a grandiose gallery – it was all a dazzling display to him. At one glance he saw so many venerable elderly and not-so-elderly gentlemen with stars on their tailcoats, ladies stepping forward so lightly and gracefully onto the parquet floor or sitting in rows, he heard so many French and English words, besides the young men in tailcoats were so full of nobility, they spoke or kept silent with such dignity, they were so incapable of saying anything superfluous, they joked so grandly, they smiled so courteously, they wore such stunning side whiskers, they knew how to show off their perfect hands so skilfully as they adjusted their cravats, the ladies were so airy, so engrossed in utter self-delight and rapture, they lowered their gaze so charmingly that… but Piskarev's meek look, as he leant against a column in fear, was proof enough that he had completely lost his head. At that moment the crowd clustered around a group of dancers. They darted along, wrapped in diaphanous Paris creations, gowns woven from thin air. They casually brushed the parquet floor with their sparkling little feet and they were all the more ethereal for seeming not to touch the floor at all. But one of them was even more finely, more sumptuously and more brilliantly dressed than the rest. An inexpressible, most exquisite fusion of tastes flowed throughout her attire, and yet it felt as though she had not taken care of it herself, as though it had just happened. She looked both at and away from the crowd of spectators surrounding her, she lowered her beautiful long eyelashes with indifference, and the brilliant whiteness of her face was even more dazzling to the eyes when, as she inclined her head, a faint shadow spread over her charming brow.

Piskarev did his utmost to separate the crowd to get a good look at her but, to his huge annoyance, someone's large head

with dark curly hair kept on getting in the way. And he was so
squeezed by the throng that he did not risk moving forwards
or backwards for fear of accidentally jostling some privy councillor. But he managed to edge his way through and checked
his clothes, wanting to tidy himself up. Good God, what was
this! He was wearing a frock coat smudged all over with paint:
when he had hurried out he had even forgotten to change into
something decent. He turned crimson and, dropping his head,
just wanted to disappear, but there was definitely nowhere to
disappear to: *Kammerjunkers** in shiny suits formed a complete
wall behind him. By now he really wanted to be as far away
as possible from the beautiful woman with the lovely brow
and eyelashes. He looked up in alarm to see whether she was
looking at him: my God, she stood right in front of him... But
what was this? What *was* this? "It's her!" he cried out almost
at the top of his voice. It was her indeed, the very woman he
had met on Nevsky Prospect and had escorted to her place.

Meanwhile, she had raised her eyelashes and glanced
around with her clear gaze. "Oh, oh, how lovely she is!"
was all he could say, catching his breath. She looked round
the circle of people who were all vying for her attention,
but she soon turned her gaze away somewhat wearily and
absent-mindedly and met Piskarev's eyes. Oh, Heavens! Oh
Paradise! Give him strength to bear this, Lord! Life can't
take this; his soul will be destroyed and removed! She gave

a signal, not with her hand, not with an inclination of her head – no, her stunning eyes conveyed this signal in such a subtle, imperceptible way that no one else could see it; yet he saw it, he understood it. The dance went on for a long time: the jaded music seemed to be flagging and petering out, but then it would erupt again and screech and thunder. The end at last! She sat down, her bosom heaving beneath the flimsy gauze; her hand (God, what a lovely hand!) slipped to her lap, crushed her fine-spun dress under it, and the dress began to breathe music, it seemed, and its fine lilac colour highlighted the striking whiteness of that lovely hand even more. Could he but touch it – nothing more! No other desires – they were all too bold... He stood behind her chair, not daring to speak, not daring to breathe.

"Were you bored?" she said. "So was I. I notice that you hate me..." she added, lowering her long eyelashes.

"Hate you! Me? I..." began Piskarev, now in a complete panic, and he would probably have come out with a string of unintelligible words, but at that moment a chamberlain approached, with witty and pleasant remarks and a beautifully twisted topknot on his head. He quite pleasantly flashed a row of rather good teeth and with each witticism drove a sharp nail into Piskarev's heart. At last, fortunately, someone else turned to the chamberlain with some query.

"How unbearable this is!" she said, raising her divine eyes towards him. "I'll go and sit down at the other end of the room. Be there!"

She stole through the crowd and vanished. He pushed his way like a madman through the crowd and was already there.

It was her indeed! She was seated like a tsarina, better and lovelier than everyone else, and she was seeking him out with her eyes.

"You're here," she spoke softly. "I'll be honest with you: you probably found the circumstances under which we met rather strange. Can you even think that I could belong to that despicable class of creatures among whom you met me? My behaviour seems strange to you, but I'll tell you a secret – will you be able," she said fixing him with her eyes, "never to betray it?"

"Oh, I will! I will! I will!…"

But just then a rather elderly gentleman came up and said something to her in some language incomprehensible to Piskarev and offered her his arm. She looked pleadingly at Piskarev and motioned him to stay where he was and to wait for her return, but in a fit of impatience he was incapable of obeying any orders even from her lips. He followed her, but the crowd separated them. He could no longer see her lilac dress; he anxiously went from room to room and bumped callously into everyone in his way, but in every room there were some bigwigs playing whist, plunged in deathly silence. In the corner of one room some elderly men argued about the advantages of military service over civil service; in another corner gentlemen in very smart tailcoats made light-hearted observations about the multi-volumed publications of some hard-working poet. Piskarev felt one respectable-looking elderly gentleman grab him by the button of his tailcoat and submit an entirely reasonable observation to his judgement, but he roughly pushed him aside without even noticing that the gentleman wore a rather important medal round his neck. He ran across to the next room – she was not there either. Nor in a third room. "Where is she? Give her to me! Oh, I can't live without seeing her! I want to hear what she wanted to tell me." Yet all his searching was in vain. Anxious and exhausted, he squashed himself into a corner and watched the crowd, but to his strained eyes everything began to appear rather blurred. Finally the walls of his own room began to emerge distinctly. He raised his eyes: before him stood the candlestick with the flame almost spent in its hollow; the candle had completely burnt down and the tallow spilt on the table.

So he'd been asleep! God, what a dream! And why did he have to wake up? Why had it not lasted one minute longer: she would surely have reappeared! Tiresome daylight looked in through his window with its unpleasant feeble glow. His room was such a grey, murky mess... Oh, how loathsome reality was! What was it compared to dreams? He quickly undressed and lay on his bed; he wrapped himself up in his blanket, wishing to conjure up, even for an instant, his disappearing dream. Sleep was in fact not slow in coming, but it did not offer him at all what he wanted to see: at one moment Lieutenant Pirogov came to view with his pipe, the next a porter of the Academy, then an actual state councillor, then the head of a Finnish woman whose portrait he had once painted, and similar nonsense.

He lay in bed right up to midday, longing to drop off again, but she did not appear. If he could only behold her beautiful features for a moment, hear the sound of her light footsteps and catch a glimpse of her bare arm, gleaming like heavenly snow.

Utterly detached and oblivious to everything, he sat grief-stricken and forlorn, filled solely with that one dream. He had no thoughts of reaching out for anything. His eyes, impassive and lifeless, gazed through the window overlooking the court-yard, where a dirty gutter dripped water that froze in mid-air and the pedlar's goat-like voice bleated: "Old clothes for sale!" His hearing was strangely affected by all humdrum everyday occurrences. He sat this way until evening and eagerly threw himself back onto his bed. He struggled a long time with sleeplessness, but finally overcame it. Again just some dream, some trivial, vile dream. "God, have mercy: show her to me, if just for one moment, one single moment!" Again he waited for evening, again fell asleep, again dreamt of some clerk – who was both a clerk and a bassoon at the same time. Oh, this was unbearable! At last she appeared! Her little head and curls... she looks... Oh, how brief a moment! And again mist, again some stupid dream.

In the end he lived for his dreams, and from that time on his whole existence took a strange turn: it could be said that he slept in his waking hours and kept awake in his sleep. If someone had seen him sitting in silence at an empty table or walking down the street, then he would no doubt have taken him for a lunatic or a man destroyed by hard drink. His gaze held no meaning at all; in the end his innate absent-mindedness took over and resolutely drove all feeling, all movement from his face. He only came to life as night fell.

This state of affairs depleted his strength, and what tormented him most was that in the end sleep began to abandon him entirely. Wanting to save this one remaining luxury, he used all his powers to restore it. He had heard that there was a way of restoring sleep – you only had to take opium for that to happen. But where to get hold of some? He recalled a Persian who ran a shawl shop, and who, whenever they met, almost invariably asked him to paint a beautiful girl for him. He decided to go to him, assuming that he was bound to have opium. The Persian received him seated cross-legged on a divan.

"What do you want opium for?" he asked.

Piskarev told him about his insomnia.

"Fine, I'll give you opium, but you must paint a beautiful girl for me. Make her a real beauty! Let her have dark eyebrows and eyes as big as olives; and let me be lying beside her smoking my pipe! Do you hear? Make her beautiful! Make her a beauty!"

Piskarev promised the lot. The Persian went out for a moment and returned with a small jar filled with a dark liquid, carefully poured some of it into another small jar and handed it over to Piskarev, instructing him not to take more than seven drops in water. He greedily grabbed this precious jar, which he would not have given up for a pile of gold, and rushed home.

Back home he poured a few drops in a glass of water, gulped it down and collapsed into bed.

God, what bliss! It's her! Her again! But this time in a completely different guise. Oh, how sweetly she sits by the window of a bright little country cottage. Her dress exudes a simplicity that matches only a poet's vision. Her hair... O Lord, how simply her hair is done up and how it suits her! A small scarf is lightly thrown round her slender neck; everything about her is chaste, everything conveys a mysterious, indescribable sense of taste. How sweet her graceful gait! What music in the sound of her footsteps and the rustle of her simple dress! How lovely her arm, clasped by a horsehair bracelet! She speaks to him with tears in her eyes: "Don't despise me: I'm not at all what you take me for. Look at me, take a good look and tell me: am I really capable of what you think?"

"Oh, no, no! Let anyone who dares think that, let him…"

But he woke up, deeply moved, tormented, with tears in his eyes. "It would be better if you didn't exist at all! If you were not alive, but only the creation of an inspired artist! I wouldn't move away from the canvas, I'd forever look at you and kiss you. I'd live and breathe through you, like a most wonderful dream, and I'd be happy. I wouldn't reach out for anything else. I'd summon you, like a guardian angel, before sleep and in my waking hours, and would wait for you when I wanted to portray the divine and the sacred. But now, what a terrible life is mine! What's the use of her being alive? Can the life of a madman be pleasant for relatives and friends who once cared for him? My God, what a life! A constant struggle between dreams and reality!" Thoughts more or less like these constantly absorbed him. He thought of nothing else and hardly ate – and, with a lover's passion, impatiently waited for the evening to come, and with it the longed-for vision. This constant focus on just this one thing in the end so dominated his daily life and his imagination that the longed-for image appeared to him almost daily, always in a situation totally opposed to reality, since his thoughts were completely pure, like those of a child. Through these dreams the object itself became purer somehow and underwent a complete transformation.

The doses of opium inflamed his thoughts even more, and if there ever was a man besotted, impetuously, desperately, destructively, frenziedly, to the ultimate degree of madness, then he was that unfortunate man.

Of all his dreams there was one that brought him more joy than all the rest: it took place in his studio; he was so happy and sat with such delight, palette in hand! And she was there too. She was his wife by now. She sat beside him, resting her charming elbow on the back of his chair and looking at his work. Her languorous, drowsy eyes expressed the fullness of bliss. Everything in his room breathed of paradise: it was so bright, so neat. Lord! She leant her adorable little head on his chest... He had never had a more wonderful dream. After that he got up more light-hearted and less abstracted than before. Strange thoughts came to him. "Perhaps," he thought, "she has been drawn into debauchery by some terrible circumstance beyond her control; perhaps her soul's impulses are inclined towards repentance; perhaps she herself longs to break away from her terrible situation. So should I thoughtlessly allow her to be destroyed, and particularly when all that's needed is to reach out to save her from drowning?" His thoughts went further still. "No one knows me," he said to himself. "Who should be concerned about me when I'm not concerned about anyone myself? If she expresses real remorse and changes her life, then I'll marry her. I must marry her, and I'm bound to do better than many who marry their housekeepers or often the most despicable creatures. But my gesture will be selfless and perhaps even magnanimous. I'll be returning to the world its most beautiful adornment."

Having hatched such a foolish plan, he felt his face turn red; he walked over to the mirror and scared himself at the sight of his sunken cheeks and the pallor of his face. He carefully began to smarten himself up; he washed, sleeked down his hair, put on a new tailcoat and a dapper waistcoat, threw on a cloak and went out. He breathed in the fresh air and felt freshness in his heart like a convalescent who has decided to go out for the first time after a protracted illness. His heart was pounding as he approached the street he had not set foot on since that fatal encounter.

He searched a long time for the house; it seemed his memory had failed him. He walked the length of the street twice and did not know in front of which house to stop. At last one house seemed to look right. He swiftly ran up the stairs, knocked at the door: the door opened, and who should come towards him? His ideal, his mysterious image, the original picture of his dreams, the one through whom he lived – lived so desperately, so painfully, so sweetly. She stood before him: he began to tremble – he could hardly stay upright from weakness while transported with joy. She stood before him, just as beautiful: although her eyes were sleepy, although a pallor had crept onto her face, no longer as fresh as before, yet she was still beautiful.

"Ah!" she exclaimed, having caught sight of Piskarev and then rubbing her eyes (it was already two o'clock by then). "Why did you run away from us that time?"

He sat down ready to drop and gazed at her.

"I've only just woken up; I was taken home at seven this morning. I was completely drunk," she added with a smile.

Oh, better you were dumb, altogether without speech, rather than say such things! She suddenly displayed her whole life to him, as in a panorama. He nevertheless decided with a sinking heart to see whether his exhortations would make any impression on her. Pulling himself together, he began to point out to her in a trembling but also impassioned voice the terrible situation she was in. She listened to him intently and with that feeling of amazement we express when confronted with something unexpected and strange. She glanced with a faint smile at her friend, who sat in a corner and who, having stopped cleaning out her comb, was listening closely to this new preacher.

"I'm poor, it's true," Piskarev said at last after a long and edifying exhortation, "but we'll set to work; we'll vie with each other as we strive to improve our lives. There's nothing nicer than to be beholden only to oneself. I'll sit and paint, you'll sit beside me, inspire me in my work and embroider or do some other needlework, and we'll want for nothing."

"Well really!" she said, interrupting his flow with something of contempt. "I'm not a laundress or a seamstress who needs to take up work."

God! Her whole miserable, contemptible life was conveyed in those words – a life full of frivolity and idleness, true partners in depravity.

"Marry me!" her friend, who had so far remained silent in her corner, pitched in with an impudent look. "If I were a wife, this is how I'd sit!"

And with that she put on some kind of silly expression on her pitiful face, which amused the beauty no end.

Oh, this was just too much! It was beyond endurance. He rushed off, devoid of all feeling and thought. His mind became blurred. He roamed the streets all day, like a fool, aimlessly, not seeing, hearing or feeling a thing. No one knew if he found somewhere to sleep. Only the next day some kind of dim instinct led him to his apartment, pale, haggard, dishevelled, with signs of insanity on his face. He locked himself into his room, allowed no one in and asked for nothing. Four days went by without his door being opened once. In the end a week went by and his room was still locked. People hurled themselves at the door, began to call out to him, but there was no answer. They broke down the door at last and found his lifeless body with his throat cut. A bloodstained razor lay on the floor. You could conclude from his frantically sprawling arms and his horribly

36

distorted face that his hand had been unsteady and that he had suffered for a long time before his sinful soul left his body.

Thus perished a victim of mad passion, poor Piskarev, quiet, timid, unassuming, with the candour of a child, carrying within him the spark of a talent that might in time have blazed brightly far and wide. No one shed a tear for him; no one was to be seen by his lifeless body except for the usual presence of the district inspector and the detached countenance of the town doctor. They took his coffin quietly to Okhta, without even any religious rites; of those who followed him only one military guard wept, and then only because he had drunk an extra measure of vodka. Even Lieutenant Pirogov did not come to see the body of the poor wretch, to whom when alive he had lent his lofty patronage. Anyway, he had no time for this at all: he was involved in an extraordinary event. Let's rather turn to him.

I don't like corpses and dead people, and always resent coming across a long funeral procession when a disabled veteran, dressed up as some kind of Capuchin, takes snuff with his left hand because his right arm is holding a torch. And I'm always deeply annoyed at the sight of an opulent hearse and velvet-covered coffin; but this annoyance is compounded with sadness when I see a carter dragging a pauper's uncovered pine coffin with only some beggar woman, who chanced upon it at a crossroads, trudging along behind him with nothing better to do.

I believe that we left Lieutenant Pirogov at the point when he took leave of poor Piskarev and dashed off after the blonde girl. This blonde was a dainty, fairly interesting little thing. She would stop in front of every shop and gape at the sashes, scarves, earrings, gloves and other trinkets on display in the windows, constantly twisting and turning and staring in all directions, then glancing back again. "You, little darling, are mine!" Pirogov said self-assuredly, as he continued to pursue her, and he hid his face with his coat collar to avoid meeting anyone he knew. But I'd better tell the readers who this Pirogov was.

But before telling you who this Lieutenant Pirogov was, it would be better to say something about the kind of society Pirogov belonged to. There are officers in St Petersburg who form some kind of middle class within its society. You will always find one of those at a soirée or dinner at the home of a state councillor or even of an actual state councillor, who has qualified for that rank by dint of forty years of service. Several pale daughters, completely insipid like St Petersburg itself, some of them past their prime, the tea table, the piano, dancing – all of this was inseparable from the bright epaulette shining in the lamplight, between the well-behaved blonde and the black tailcoat of a brother or family friend. It is extremely hard to rouse these cold-blooded maidens or even to make them laugh: great skill is needed to achieve this, or even better, no skill at all. You have to express yourself neither too cleverly nor too amusingly, so that everything remains trivial, which is what women love. Here one must give the gentlemen in question their due. They are particularly adept at making these colourless beauties laugh and listen. Cries and strangled laughter such as: "Oh, do stop! Shame on you for making me laugh so!" are often their best reward. They are very rarely found in high society or, more accurately, they never are. They are totally excluded from there by those whom this society calls aristocrats. By the way, they are considered knowledgeable and well-educated people. They enjoy chatting about literature; they praise Bulgarin, Pushkin and Grech, and they speak scornfully and make caustic remarks about A.A. Orlov.* They do not miss a single public lecture, be it about bookkeeping or even forestry. At the theatre, whatever the play, you will find one of them, except when they are showing one of the Filatkas,* which greatly offends their discerning taste. They are always at the theatre. They are the most desirable people for stage directors. They particularly like good verses in a play; they also enjoy calling out loudly for the actors. Several of them, who teach in state institutions or prepare students for entrance to those institutions, finally acquire a cabriolet and a pair of horses. At that stage their circle widens; they at last reach the point when they can marry a merchant's daughter who can play the piano and has around one hundred thousand in cash and a collection of bearded relatives. Yet they cannot attain that honour before they have reached the rank of colonel at the very least. Because under no circumstance will those Russian bearded merchants, despite still giving off a faint whiff of cabbage, see any daughter of theirs marry anyone below the rank of general, or a colonel at the very least. Such are the main characteristics of this kind of young man. But Lieutenant Pirogov had a multitude of talents that were his alone. He was superb at declaiming verses from *Dmitry Donskoy* and *Woe from Wit*,* and he was so skilful at blowing smoke rings from his pipe that he could string them one after another, up to ten in one go. He had a very pleasing way of telling the anecdote about the cannon being one thing and the unicorn being another.* It is quite hard, however, to enumerate all the talents fate had bestowed on Pirogov. He enjoyed talking about some actress or dancer, but not as bluntly as a young ensign would express himself on the subject. He was very pleased with his rank, to which he had recently been promoted, and although sometimes, when lounging on a sofa, he would say: "Oh, oh! It's vanity, all is vanity! So what if I'm a lieutenant?" he was secretly hugely flattered by this new status. In conversation he would often try to drop indirect hints – and once, when he bumped in the street into some clerk who seemed disrespectful to him, he immediately stopped him and in a few sharp words gave him to understand that this was not just any officer standing before him but a lieutenant. And he tried to elaborate on this even more eloquently when at that moment two rather attractive ladies were passing by. Pirogov on the whole displayed a passion for everything refined, and encouraged the artist Piskarev. However, this was perhaps because he very much wished to behold his manly countenance in a portrait. But enough about Pirogov's qualities. Man is such an amazing creature that it is impossible to list all his virtues at once and the more you look the more new distinctive features appear, and describing them would be an endless task.

And so Pirogov did not give up pursuing the unknown girl, now and then putting a question to her, to which she replied sharply and abruptly, muttering incoherently. They went through the dark Kazan Gates into Meshchanskaya Street, a street of tobacconists and other small shops, of German craftsmen and Finnish nymphs. The blonde girl hurried on and darted through the gates of a rather squalid house. Pirogov followed her. She ran up a narrow dark stairway and went through a door, with Pirogov boldly sneaking in after her. He found himself in a large room with black walls and a blackened ceiling. A heap of metal screws, locksmith's tools, shiny coffee pots and candlesticks were on the table; the floor was littered with iron and copper filings. Pirogov immediately realized that this was a craftsman's apartment. The unknown girl rushed on through a side door. He was about to give it a moment's consideration, but in true Russian style he decided to go on. He entered a room totally different from the previous one: very neatly kept, proof that the owner was German. He was struck by an extraordinarily strange sight. Before him sat Schiller – not the Schiller who wrote *Wilhelm Tell* and *The History of the Thirty-Year War*, but the renowned Schiller, a tinsmith in Meshchanskaya Street. Next to Schiller sat Hoffmann – not the writer Hoffmann, but a rather good shoemaker from Ofitserskaya Street, a great friend of Schiller's. Schiller was drunk and sitting on a chair, stamping his foot and heatedly holding forth. All this would not really have surprised Pirogov: what did surprise him was the extremely strange position the men's bodies were in. Schiller sat with his rather bulbous nose sticking out and his head raised, while Hoffmann held him by that nose with two fingers, twisting the blade of his shoemaker's knife over its surface. Both individuals spoke German, which is why Lieutenant Pirogov, whose knowledge of German consisted only of "*Gut Morgen*", couldn't understand a thing of what was going on. By the way, Schiller's words were the following:

"I don't want, I don't need a nose!" he said, waving his arms about. "On my nose alone I spend three pounds of snuff every month. And I pay in a horrid Russian shop, because the German shop doesn't sell Russian tobacco, and in that horrid Russian shop I pay forty copecks for each pound of tobacco – this means one rouble and twenty copecks: twelve times one rouble and twenty copecks comes to fourteen roubles and forty copecks! And on holidays I sniff *rapé*,* because on holidays I don't want to sniff horrible Russian tobacco. I sniff two pounds of *rapé* a year at two roubles a pound. Six and fourteen – twenty roubles and forty copecks for tobacco alone. That's daylight robbery! I ask you, my dear friend Hoffmann, isn't that so?"

Hoffmann, who himself was drunk, agreed with him: "Twenty roubles and forty copecks! I'm a German from Swabia: in Germany there's a king. I don't want a nose! Cut off my nose! Here's my nose!"

And had it not been for Lieutenant Pirogov's sudden appearance, there is no doubt that Hoffmann would have cut off Schiller's nose for no apparent reason, because he held his knife in such a way as if ready to cut out a shoe sole.

Schiller found it very off-putting that an unknown, unbidden face was all of a sudden so inopportunely interfering with him. Although he was delightfully intoxicated with beer and wine, he felt that there was something unseemly about being in this state and acting this way in the presence of an outside witness. Pirogov, meanwhile, gave a small bow and said in his usual pleasant way:

"Please excuse me..."

"Clear off!" Schiller drawled.

This puzzled Lieutenant Pirogov. Such treatment was completely new to him. A faint attempt at a smile suddenly

43

disappeared from his face. With a feeling of hurt pride he said:

"I find this strange, my good sir... You probably haven't noticed... I'm an officer..."

"What officer! I am from Swabia. Myself" – Schiller hit the table with his fist – "will be an officer: one and half year a *Junker*, two years a lieutenant and tomorrow right away an officer. But I don't want to serve. I to an officer do so: pfff!" And with that Schiller raised his palm and blew on it.

Lieutenant Pirogov saw that there was nothing left for him to do but leave. However, such conduct, not at all mindful of his rank, upset him. He stopped a few times on the stairs as though to pluck up courage and find a way to make Schiller aware of his insolent behaviour. He finally considered that Schiller could be forgiven because his head was befuddled with beer. Besides, the pretty little blonde came to mind and he decided to consign all this to oblivion.

Early next morning Lieutenant Pirogov appeared in the master tinsmith's workshop. He was met in the front room by the pretty blonde, and she asked in a rather stern voice, which suited her little face very well:

"What can I do for you?"

"Oh, good morning my sweet! Don't you recognize me? You sly little one, what lovely eyes!" and with this Lieutenant Pirogov wanted to lift her chin very amiably with his finger.

But the blonde gave a cry of alarm and, just as sternly as before, said:

"What can I do for you?"

"I just want to see you; I don't need anything else," Lieutenant Pirogov said, smiling quite pleasantly and moving closer. But when he saw that the alarmed blonde girl wanted to sneak away through the door, he added:

"My sweet one, I need to order some spurs. Can you make me spurs? Although to love you it's not spurs at all that are needed, but rather a bridle. What adorable little hands!"

Lieutenant Pirogov was always very gracious when making that kind of declaration.

"I'll call my husband right now," shrieked the German girl and went out, and a few moments later Pirogov saw Schiller come out with sleepy eyes, having barely recovered from his hangover. Glancing at the officer, he recalled as in a blurred dream the events of the previous day. He had no recollection of what it had been like, but felt that he had done something foolish, which is why he received the officer with a very stern look.

"I can't take less than fifteen roubles for the spurs," he said, wanting to get rid of Pirogov because he felt most ashamed, as an honest German, to look at anyone who had seen him in such a disgraceful condition. Schiller liked to drink with two or three friends, without witnesses, and during that time he even locked himself away from his workers.

"Why so expensive?" Pirogov asked gently.

"German workmanship," Schiller said coolly, stroking his chin. "Russian will take two roubles."

"All right. To prove that I like you and want to get to know you, I'll pay fifteen roubles."

Schiller gave it a moment's thought: being an honest German, he felt somewhat ashamed. Wanting to put him off the order he explained that he could not get it done in less than two weeks. But Pirogov readily agreed without protest.

The German thought about it and began to work out in his mind how best to make the job really be worth fifteen roubles. Meanwhile the blonde came into the workshop and began to rummage around on the table, covered with coffee pots. The lieutenant took advantage of Schiller's absorption, went over to her and pressed her arm, which was bare up to the shoulder. This infuriated Schiller.

"*Mein Frau!*"* he shouted.

"*Was wollen Sie doch?*"* replied the blonde.

"*Gehen Sie* to kitchen!"

The blonde withdrew.

"So in two weeks' time?" said Pirogov.

"Yes, in two weeks' time," replied Schiller absent-mindedly. "I have a lot of work right now."

"Goodbye! I'll be back then."

"Goodbye," replied Schiller, locking the door behind him.

Lieutenant Pirogov resolved not to give up on his quest, despite the fact that the German blonde had blatantly rebuffed him. He could not understand how anyone could resist him, the more so because his amiability and his splendid rank gave him the right to be noticed. It must be said, however, that Schiller's wife, for all her sweet looks, was very stupid. Though stupidity adds a particular charm to a pretty wife. At least I've known many husbands who are enraptured by their wives' stupidity and see in it the signs of childish innocence. Beauty works true miracles. All mental shortcomings in a beautiful woman, rather than provoking disgust, become unusually attractive somehow: vice itself comes in the guise of prettiness. But if good looks disappear, then a woman needs to be twenty times cleverer than a man to inspire, if not love, then at least respect. Schiller's wife, however, for all her foolishness, was always faithful to her duties, and it would be quite hard for Pirogov to succeed in his bold undertaking – but there is always pleasure in overcoming obstacles, and the blonde became more interesting to him day by day. He began to come quite frequently to enquire about the spurs, to the point of really annoying Schiller. He did all he could to finish the spurs, and it was done at last.

"Oh, what superb workmanship!" Lieutenant Pirogov exclaimed when he saw the spurs. "Lord, how beautifully made! Even our general doesn't have such spurs."

A glow of self-satisfaction spread through Schiller. His eyes began to look quite cheerful, and he was completely reconciled with Pirogov. "The Russian officer is a clever man," he thought to himself.

"Can you make a sheath, for example, for a dagger or other things?"

"I certainly can," said Schiller, smiling.

"Then make me a sheath for my dagger. I'll bring it to you: I have a very beautiful Turkish dagger, but I'd like a different sheath for it."

Schiller could have been hit by a bomb. He suddenly screwed up his face. "You asked for that!" he thought, cursing inwardly for having made more work for himself. By now he considered it dishonourable to refuse and, besides, the Russian officer had praised his workmanship. He agreed, after some head- shaking, but the kiss which Pirogov, on his way out, brazenly planted on the very lips of the pretty blonde threw him into complete bewilderment.

It would not be unreasonable, I think, to introduce Schiller a little more closely to the reader. Schiller was a true German in the full sense of the word. At the age of twenty, that happy time when a Russian lives just as he pleases, Schiller had already mapped out his whole life, without making exceptions for anyone or anything. He made it a rule to get up at seven, dine at two, be precise in everything he did and get drunk on

Sundays. He resolved that within ten years he would raise a capital of 50,000 roubles, and this was as assured and irrefutable as fate, because it is more likely for a clerk to forget to call in at the porter's lodge of his superior than it is for a German to go back on his word. Under no circumstance did he increase his expenses, and if the price of potatoes went up more than usual, he would not add another copeck, but would decrease the quantity, and though he sometimes went a bit hungry, he just got used to it. This precision even extended to kissing his wife no more than twice every twenty-four hours and, to stop himself kissing her inadvertently an extra time, he never put more than one teaspoon of pepper in his soup. However, on Sundays this rule was not so strictly adhered to, because Schiller then drank two bottles of beer and one of caraway vodka, which he nevertheless persistently cursed. He did not drink at all like an Englishman, who bolts the door straight after dinner and gets drunk all on his own. On the contrary, being German, he always drank wholeheartedly, either in the company of Hoffmann the shoemaker, or with Kunz the carpenter, who was also German and a heavy drinker. Such was the character of the honourable Schiller, who was finally put in an extremely awkward position. Although he was phlegmatic and German, Pirogov's behaviour aroused in him something akin to jealousy. He racked his brain, but could not come up with a way of getting rid of that Russian officer. Pirogov, meanwhile, smoking his pipe in the company of his friends – because Providence had ordained that where there were officers, there were pipes – and so, smoking his pipe in the company of his friends, gave meaningful hints with a genial smile about a little intrigue involving a pretty German woman with whom, in his own words, he was on rather intimate terms, yet whom in reality he had almost lost hope of winning over.

One day he was strolling along Meshchanskaya Street glancing up at the house with Schiller's shop sign advertising coffee pots and samovars. To his huge delight he caught sight of the blonde's head, leaning out of the window and watching the passers-by. He stopped, blew her a kiss and said: "*Gut Morgen*!" The blonde greeted him as an acquaintance.

"Is your husband home?"

"He is," the blonde replied.

"And when is he not at home?"

"He's away on Sundays," said the silly blonde.

"That's not bad," Pirogov mused. "I must make the most of that."

And the following Sunday he appeared out of the blue before the blonde. Schiller was indeed not at home. The pretty lady of the house was startled, but this time Pirogov trod rather carefully, behaved very respectfully and, when bowing, he flaunted the full beauty of his supple, closely fitted waist. His banter was very pleasant and courteous, but the silly German girl only replied in monosyllables. In the end, having tried everything and seeing that nothing caught her interest, he asked her to dance. The German girl immediately agreed, because German women are always very fond of dancing. Pirogov based much hope in this: firstly it was something she already liked; secondly, it would show off his posture and his dexterity, and thirdly, when dancing, he could get much closer and embrace the pretty German girl and bring about the desired effect – in short, he expected to achieve complete success. He began with a kind of gavotte, knowing that German women needed a gentle start. The pretty German girl stepped to the middle of the room and raised her lovely little foot. This position threw Pirogov into such raptures that he rushed to kiss her. The German girl began to scream, and this only added to her charm in Pirogov's eyes: he covered her in kisses. Suddenly the door opened and in came Schiller with Hoffmann and Kunz the carpenter. All those worthy craftsmen were as drunk as skunks.

But I'll leave my readers to judge for themselves Schiller's anger and indignation.

"You rascal!" he screamed in a fury. "How dare you kiss my wife? You're a scoundrel, not a Russian officer. Damn it, my friend Hoffmann, I'm a German, not a Russian swine!"

Hoffmann concurred.

"Oh, I won't wear the horns! Grab him, my friend Hoffmann, by the collar! I won't!" he went on, his arms flailing and his face as red as the fabric of his waistcoat. "I live eight years in St Petersburg, I have my mother in Swabia and an uncle in Nuremberg. I'm a German and not a horned piece of beef! Get everything off him, my friend Hoffmann! Hold him down by arms and legs, my comrade Kunz!"

And the Germans grabbed Pirogov by his arms and legs.

He tried in vain to beat them off. Those three craftsmen were the heftiest German fellows of all St Petersburg and dealt with him so roughly and disrespectfully that, I confess, I cannot find the words to describe this sorry event.

I'm convinced that the following day found Schiller in a high fever, that he shook like a leaf expecting the police to arrive at any minute, and that he would have given God knows what for the events of the previous day to have been but a dream. But there's no changing what has been. Nothing could equal Pirogov's fury and indignation. The very thought of that appalling outrage drove him mad. Siberia and a flogging seemed the very least punishment for Schiller. He flew home to dress and from there go straight on to the General, to give him the most lurid account of the German craftsmen's riotous conduct. He also wanted to submit a written appeal to Staff Headquarters at once. If Staff Headquarters imposed an inadequate punishment, then he would go straight to the State Council or else to the Tsar himself.

But it all ended rather oddly: along the way he called into a patisserie, ate two puff pastries, read something or other in

The Northern Bee* and by the time he left he was not as angry as before. Besides, quite a pleasant cool breeze impelled him to go for a stroll along Nevsky Prospect. By nine o'clock he had calmed down and found that it was not a good thing to disturb the General on a Sunday, and besides, he would surely have been summoned somewhere; and so he went off to a soirée given by the Director of the Board of Control, where there was an extremely pleasant gathering of civil servants and officers. He spent a very enjoyable evening there and so distinguished himself when dancing the mazurka that he enchanted not only the ladies but also their partners.

"Marvellous how our world is fashioned!" I thought as I walked along Nevsky Prospect a couple of days ago, recalling those two incidents. "How strangely, how mystifyingly does our fate toy with us! Do we ever obtain what we desire? Do we ever achieve what our own powers seem to be deliberately conditioned for? Everything happens the wrong way round. Fate has given one person beautiful horses, on which he rides nonchalantly without even noticing their beauty, whilst another, whose heart burns with a passion for horses, goes on foot and contents himself with clicking his tongue when a trotter is led by. One has an excellent cook but unfortunately such a small mouth that it cannot accommodate more than two morsels at one time. Another has a mouth as big as the arch of Staff Headquarters, but alas has to content himself with some kind of German dinner consisting of potatoes. How strangely does our fate toy with us!"

But the most bizarre incidents of all are those that occur on Nevsky Prospect. Oh, don't trust this Nevsky Prospect! I always wrap myself up a little tighter in my cloak when I walk along it and try to avoid looking at anything I encounter. It's all deception, dreams – nothing is what it seems! You think this gentleman who walks by in a beautifully tailored frock coat is very wealthy? Not a bit of it: he consists entirely of that one coat. You think that those two stout gentlemen who have stopped in front of a church under construction are deliberating its architectural merits? Not at all: they're talking about the strange way two crows are sitting facing one another. You think this gesticulating enthusiast is speaking of how his wife threw a little ball out of the window at an officer, a complete stranger? Absolutely not: he's speaking of Lafayette. You think that these ladies... but trust ladies even less! Stare less at shop windows: the trinkets laid out there are pretty, but they carry the smell of a horrifying number of banknotes. God preserve you from peeping beneath a lady's hat! However much a beautiful lady's cloak flutters in the distance, I'll not pursue her at any price to get a closer look. Move away, for Heaven's sake, from the street lamp! And go faster, go past it as fast as you can. You'll be lucky to get away with only its fetid oil spilling over your fashionable frock coat. Everything, along with the street lamp, breathes deceit. It lies at any time of day, this Nevsky Prospect, but most of all it lies when night cloaks it with its thick layer and picks out the white and pale-yellow walls of the houses, when the whole city turns into boom and glitter, myriads of carriages spill down from the bridges, postilions shout and bounce up and down on their horses, and when the Devil himself lights the street lamps solely to disclose everything, but not as it really is.

The Nose

I

O N 25TH MARCH an extraordinarily odd incident took place in St Petersburg. The barber Ivan Yakovlevich, who lives on Vosnesensky Avenue – his surname has been lost and, even on his shop sign, which depicts a gentleman with a lathered cheek and an inscription: "We do bloodletting too", there is no other information – so, the barber Ivan Yakovlevich woke up rather early and detected the smell of hot bread. Raising himself up slightly in bed, he saw his wife, a rather respectable lady who loved drinking coffee, taking freshly baked bread out of the oven.

"Today, Praskovya Osipovna, I won't be drinking coffee," Ivan Yakovlevich said. "I really want to have some hot bread with onion instead."

(The fact is that Ivan Yakovlevich wanted both, but he also knew that it was absolutely impossible to ask for both at once, as Praskovya Osipovna did not care at all for such whims.)

"Let the fool eat bread: it suits me even better," his wife thought to herself. "It'll mean an extra cup of coffee for me." And she flung a bread roll on the table.

Ivan Yakovlevich, for decency's sake, put on a tailcoat over his shirt and, having sat down at the table, sprinkled some salt, got two onions ready, grabbed a knife and, with a solemn look, began to cut the bread. When he had cut the bread in two halves, he glanced in the middle and, to his surprise saw some whitish object. Ivan Yakovlevich poked at it carefully with his knife and felt it with his finger. "It's solid!" he said to himself. "What could this be?"

He stuck his fingers in and pulled out – a nose!... Ivan Yakovlevich dropped his arms; he began to rub his eyes and feel around: it was a nose, really a nose! And it also seemed somehow familiar. Ivan Yakovlevich's face expressed horror. But that horror was nothing compared to the indignation that took hold of his wife.

"Where did you cut that nose off, you brute?" she shrieked furiously. "You crook! Drunkard! I'll denounce you to the police myself. Murderer! I've heard from three men that while you're shaving you pull at their noses so hard that they can hardly cling on."

But Ivan Yakovlevich was more dead than alive. He was aware that the nose belonged to none other than the Collegiate Assessor Kovalyov,* whom he shaved on Wednesdays and Sundays.

"Stop, Praskovya Osipovna! I'll wrap it in a cloth and put it in a corner: let it lie there for a bit and I'll take it away afterwards."

"I won't hear of it! As if I'd allow a cut-off nose to lie around in the room! You dried-up old stick! All you're capable of is stropping your razor, and you soon won't be able to honour your debts at all, you slob, you scoundrel! As if I'd answer to the police because of you! Oh you boor, stupid blockhead! Get rid of it! Take it wherever you want! As long as I hear no more of it!"

Ivan Yakovlevich stood there, completely crushed. He thought and thought, but did not know what to make of it.

"The Devil knows how this happened," he said at last, scratching behind his ear. "Whether I came home drunk or not yesterday, I can't really say. All the indications are that this is just absurd: this is bread – some kind of baked thing, so definitely not a nose. I just don't get it!…"

Ivan Yakovlevich lapsed into silence. He was beside himself at the thought that the police would find the nose at his house and bring a charge against him. He already fancied he saw the scarlet collar, beautifully embroidered with silver, the sword… and he shook all over. He finally reached for his undershirt and boots, pulled on all that frippery and, accompanied by Praskovya Osipovna's robust admonitions, wrapped the nose in a rag and went out.

He wanted to shove it away somewhere, under a gatepost perhaps, or somehow inadvertently drop it and then turn down a side street. But as luck would have it he kept on bumping into one acquaintance or another who would begin to ask him: "Where are you off to?" or: "Who are you going to shave at this early hour?" – so that Ivan Yakovlevich failed to find the right moment. Another time he had actually dropped it, when a sentry guard pointed at it with his halberd from afar saying: "Pick it up! You dropped something!" And Ivan Yakovlevich had to pick up the nose and hide it in his pocket. He was overcome by despair, especially with the street steadily filling up with people, as shops and stalls began to open.

He decided to go to St Isaac's Bridge to see whether he could somehow toss it into the Neva… But I'm somewhat at fault for not having so far told you anything about Ivan Yakovlevich, a respectable man in many ways.

Ivan Yakovlevich, like any decent Russian skilled worker, was a dreadful drunkard. And although he shaved other people's chins every day, his own remained forever unshaven. Ivan Yakovlevich's tailcoat (Ivan Yakovlevich never went out in a frock coat) was piebald: in other words, it was black with brownish-yellow and grey spots. The collar was shiny, and instead of three buttons there hung only three threads. Ivan Yakovlevich was a great cynic, and whenever the Collegiate Assessor Kovalyov said to him during a shaving session: "Ivan Yakovlevich, your hands always stink!" Ivan Yakovlevich would reply with a question: "Why should they stink?"

"I don't know, my friend, but they do," the Collegiate Assessor would say, and then Ivan Yakovlevich, after taking some snuff, would lather his cheeks, under his nose and behind his ears and his chin – in a word, anywhere he felt like doing so.

This respectable citizen was by now on St Isaac's Bridge. He looked around first of all, then leant over the railing as though he was having a look below the bridge to see if there were many fish darting along, and he stealthily flung down the rag with the nose in it. He felt as though he had just shed over three hundred pounds in weight. Ivan Yakovlevich even managed a grin. Instead of setting off to shave the chins of clerks, he headed towards an establishment with a sign that read "Food and Tea" to ask for a glass of punch, when he suddenly noticed at one end of the bridge a district police officer of noble appearance, with broad side whiskers, a three-cornered hat and a sword. He went numb. Meanwhile the police officer beckoned to him with his finger saying:

"Step over here, my good man!"

Ivan Yakovlevich, knowing the form, took off his cap even from a distance, quickly went over and said:

"I wish Your Honour good health!"

"No, no, dear chap, none of that 'Your Honour'. Just tell me what you were doing there on the bridge?"

"Honestly, sir, I was on my way to shave someone, but just had a look to see if the river was flowing fast."

"You're a liar, a liar! You won't get away with that. Kindly answer!"

"I'm ready to shave Your Grace twice a week, or even three times without fail," Ivan Yakovlevich replied.

"No, my friend, that's just nonsense! I have three barbers to shave me, and they even regard it a great honour. Will you kindly tell me what you were doing there?"

Ivan Yakovlevich turned pale... But at this point the incident is completely shrouded in mist and definitely nothing is known of what happened after that.

2

COLLEGIATE ASSESSOR Kovalyov woke up rather early and went "brr..." with his lips, something he always did when he woke up, although he himself could not explain why he did this. Kovalyov stretched himself and asked for a small mirror that stood on the table to be brought to him. He wanted to check out a pimple that had popped up on his nose the previous evening, but to his huge amazement he discovered that there was a completely flat surface instead of a nose! Startled, Kovalyov asked for some water and wiped his eyes with a towel: there really was no nose there! He began feeling with his hand to make sure he was not asleep. No, he did not appear to be asleep. Collegiate Assessor Kovalyov jumped out of bed, shook himself: still no nose!... He immediately asked for his clothes and flew straight out to see the Police Superintendent.

Meanwhile something should be said about Kovalyov, so that the reader may see what kind of a person this Collegiate Assessor was. One must never compare the collegiate assessors who gain this title by means of academic certificates with those collegiate assessors who acquire it in the Caucasus.* The two are entirely different. Academic collegiate assessors... But Russia is such a strange land that if you speak of one collegiate assessor then all other collegiate assessors from Riga to Kamchatka are bound to assume that you are referring to them. The same holds true for all titles and ranks. Kovalyov was the Caucasian kind of collegiate assessor. He had only held that title for two years, and hence could not forget it for one minute, and to enhance his nobility and authority he never called himself Collegiate Assessor but always Major.* "Listen, my dear," he would say when meeting some woman selling shirt fronts on the street. "Come over to my house: my apartment is on Sadovaya Street; just ask if Major Kovalyov lives there. Anyone will show you the way." If he happened to meet a pretty little thing he would top that with a secret instruction, adding: "Just ask for Major Kovalyov's apartment, sweetie." This is why from now on we'll refer to this Collegiate Assessor as Major.

Major Kovalyov was in the habit of going every day for a stroll along Nevsky Prospect. The collar of his shirt front was always immaculate and stiffly starched. His side whiskers were of the kind you see worn to this day by provincial and district land surveyors, architects and regimental doctors, as well as by those who carry out various law-enforcement duties and generally by those men with chubby rosy cheeks who are very good at playing Boston: those side whiskers run right across the cheeks and straight up to the nose. Major Kovalyov carried a great number of cornelian seals with coats of arms and with words such as Wednesday, Thursday, Monday and so on engraved on them. Major Kovalyov had come to St Petersburg from necessity, namely to find a post in keeping with his title: if in luck, as vice-governor and, failing that, as administrator in some prominent department. Major Kovalyov was not against marriage, but only if a sum of 200,000 roubles came with the bride. And so the reader can now judge for himself what state this Major found himself in when he saw a most ridiculous flat smooth surface instead of a rather nice, average-sized nose.

As luck would have it, not a single cab driver appeared in the street, and he had to proceed on foot, wrapped in his cloak and covering his face with a handkerchief, giving the impression that he was bleeding. "But perhaps I've just imagined it: it's impossible for a nose to go stupidly missing," he thought, and stepped into a patisserie on purpose to look at himself in a mirror. Thankfully there were no customers in the patisserie; young boys were sweeping the floor and arranging the chairs. Some bleary-eyed ones carried out trays with hot pies. Yesterday's coffee-stained newspapers lay scattered on the tables and chairs. "Well, thank goodness, there's no one about," he said. "I can have a look now." He moved gingerly up to the mirror and glanced up: "Damn it, what a mess!" he spat out. "If only there were something there instead of the nose – but there's nothing!"

Biting his lips in frustration, he left the patisserie and, contrary to his usual practice, made up his mind not to look or smile at anyone. All of a sudden he stopped, as if rooted to the ground, by the entrance to a house: an inexplicable scene occurred before his eyes. A carriage drew up at the entrance porch: the doors opened and, stooping down, a gentleman in uniform jumped out and ran up the steps. Imagine Kovalyov's horror and astonishment when he recognized him as his very own nose! At this extraordinary sight everything seemed to go spinning before his eyes. He felt scarcely able to stay on his feet but, trembling all over as in a fever, he resolved at any cost to wait for the nose's return to the carriage. Two minutes later the nose did indeed come out. He was in a gold-braided uniform, with a high stand-up collar. He wore suede trousers and a sword on his side. The plumed hat indicated that he was ranked as a state councillor. It was quite clear that he was on his way to pay a visit to someone. He looked both ways, yelled at the coachman "Let's go!", got in and rode off.

Poor Kovalyov very nearly went out of his mind. He did not know what to make of such a strange event. How was it conceivable that the nose which only the day before had been on his face, unable to walk or ride anywhere, was now wearing a uniform! He ran after the carriage, which fortunately had not gone far and had stopped at Kazan Cathedral.

He hurried into the cathedral precinct, picked his way among the rows of old beggar women, their faces tightly wrapped in scarves with only two openings for the eyes – something he previously used to laugh at so much – and entered the church. There were only a few worshippers inside; they all just stood by the entrance. Kovalyov was so distressed that he could not muster the strength to pray and looked in every corner for that gentleman. He finally saw him standing apart. The nose completely hid his face behind the high collar and prayed with an expression of the greatest devotion.

"How shall I approach him?" Kovalyov thought. "It's obvious, looking at his uniform and hat, that he's a state councillor. The Devil only knows how I should go about it."

He began to cough slightly in his vicinity: not for a moment did the nose abandon his pious stance, but it continued to bow low.

"My dear sir…" Kovalyov said, steeling himself. "My dear sir…"

"What do you want?" the nose replied, turning round.

"I find it strange, my dear sir… it appears… you must know your place. And suddenly where do I find you? In church. You must agree…"

"I'm sorry, but I can't make sense of what you're saying… Please explain yourself."

"How shall I explain?" thought Kovalyov and, plucking up courage, he began:

"Of course, I… I'm a major, by the way. For me to go round without a nose, you must admit, is inappropriate. It's fine for some woman selling peeled oranges on Voskresensky Bridge to sit around without a nose. But with an eye to obtaining… and being acquainted with ladies in many houses: Chekhtareva, the State Councillor's wife and others… Judge for yourself… I don't know, my dear sir (with this Major Kovalyov shrugged his shoulders). Forgive me… if you look at it in accordance with the rules of duty and honour… you'll understand…"

"I really don't understand a thing," the nose replied. "Do explain yourself more clearly."

"My dear sir…" said Kovalyov with dignity, "I don't know how to interpret your words… The matter here seems perfectly obvious… Or do you want… You're my own nose after all!"

The nose looked at the Major and wrinkled his brow a little.

"You're mistaken, dear sir. I'm my own person. What's more, there can't be any close connection between us. Judging by the buttons on your uniform, you must be serving in another department."

Having said this, the nose turned round and went on with his prayers.

Kovalyov became totally bewildered, not knowing what to do or even think. At this point the pleasant rustle of a lady's dress reached his ears. An elderly lady, all adorned in lace, walked up, together with a slender one in a white dress, which very sweetly outlined her slim waist, and wearing a straw-coloured hat as light as puff pastry. Behind them a tall footman with huge side whiskers and dozens of collars stopped and opened a snuffbox.

Kovalyov stepped closer, pulled up the cambric collar of his shirt front, adjusted his seals hanging on a gold chain and, smiling in all directions, turned his attention to the dainty young lady who, like a spring flower, bowed slightly and lifted her white hand with its almost translucent fingers to her brow. The smile on Kovalyov's face broadened when, under her hat, he caught sight of the glowing white skin of her little rounded chin and part of her cheek tinged with the colour of an early spring rose. But all of a sudden he recoiled as though he had been burnt. He remembered that instead of a nose he had nothing at all, and tears sprung to his eyes. He turned round to accuse the gentleman in uniform outright of only pretending to be a state councillor, of being a cheat and a scoundrel and of being nothing other than his very own nose... but the nose was no longer there. He had managed to skip away, probably on another visit.

This plunged Kovalyov into despair. He walked back and stopped briefly under the colonnade, carefully looking round everywhere in case the nose came into sight. He remembered very clearly that he wore a plumed hat and a gold-braided uniform, but had failed to notice his overcoat, or the colour of his carriage, or the horses, or even whether he had a footman following him and in what livery. Besides, there were so many carriages rushing to and fro, and at such speed, that it would be hard to identify any of them. And even if he could identify one of them he would not have the means of stopping it. The day was beautiful and sunny. There were thousands of people on Nevsky Prospect. A whole flowery cascade of ladies spilt over its pavement, all the way from Politseysky Bridge to Anichkin Bridge. There went a court councillor he knew, whom he used to address as Lieutenant Colonel, especially in public. And there was Yarigin, Chief Clerk in the Senate, a close friend of his, who always lost when he bid to win eight tricks at Boston. And there was another major who had gained his assessorship in the Caucasus and who beckoned him to come over.

"Oh, to hell with it!" Kovalyov said. "Hey, driver, take me straight to the Police Superintendent!"

Kovalyov sat down in the droshky and more than once shouted at the driver: "Go like the clappers!"

"Is the Superintendent home?" he called out as he stepped into the entrance hall.

"No, he's not," the doorman replied. "He's just gone out."

"That's just great!"

"Yes," the doorman added. "It's not been that long, but he's out now. Had you come just a moment earlier you might have caught him."

Kovalyov, without removing the handkerchief from his face, got back into the droshky and yelled with despair in his voice:

"Let's go!"

"Where to?" said the driver.

"Just go straight ahead!"

"How's that, straight ahead? There's a turning coming up: right or left?"

That question stopped Kovalyov short and forced him to think again. In his situation he would do well to apply first of all to the Police Department, not because his case was a police matter, but because instructions might be followed much more speedily there than in other places. To look for satisfaction from the Heads of the Department the nose had declared himself working for was inadvisable, because it was clear from the nose's own replies that that gentleman held nothing sacred and could be lying in this case, just as he had lied when he had assured him that he had never met him before. Kovalyov was on the point of asking to be driven to the Police Department when it suddenly occurred to him that that trickster and scoundrel who had behaved so shamelessly on their first encounter could again, making good use of his time, somehow slip out of town – in which case any search would be futile – or carry on, God forbid, for a whole month. It finally seemed that Heaven itself made him see reason. He made up his mind to deal directly with a newspaper office and publish, before it was too late, a detailed description of all the nose's characteristics, so that anyone encountering him would immediately get hold of him, or at least give an idea of his whereabouts. So, having made his decision, he ordered the driver to go to the newspaper office and never stopped pummelling him in the back with his fist, all the way, saying: "Faster, you scoundrel! Faster, you rascal!"

"Hey, sir," the driver said, shaking his head and lashing his horse, whose hair was as long as that of a lapdog's. The drozhky came to a halt at last, and Kovalyov ran panting into a small reception room, where a bespectacled grey-haired clerk in an old tailcoat was seated at a desk and, holding his pen between his teeth, was counting copper coins that had been brought to him.

"Who's in charge of notices here?" shouted Kovalyov. "Ah, good day!"

"My respects," said the grey-haired clerk, briefly raising his eyes, then looking down again at the well-ordered piles of coins.

"I wish to place—"

"Be so good as to wait a moment," said the clerk, jotting down a number on a piece of paper with one hand while moving two beads on the abacus with the fingers of his left hand.

A footman with galloons and an appearance revealing that he was part of an aristocratic household stood by the desk with a note in his hand and considered it appropriate to show off his affability:

"Believe me, sir, when I say that that doggy isn't worth eighty copecks: in fact I wouldn't give eight copecks for it. But the countess loves it – my God how she loves it – and that's why there's an offer of a hundred roubles for anyone finding it! It would be right to say, between you and me, that people's tastes differ: if you're a hunter, then keep a pointer or a poodle, and then don't begrudge spending five hundred or a thousand, but make sure it's a good dog."

The worthy clerk listened to him with a knowing expression, meanwhile working out how many letters there were in the notice. A lot of old women, sales clerks and caretakers stood around holding notices. One mentioned a coachman, of sober disposition, being released for service; another a little-used carriage brought back from Paris in 1814; elsewhere a nineteen-year-old serf girl, an experienced laundress and good at other work, was on offer; a solid droshky minus one spring; a fiery young dapple-grey seventeen-year-old mare; turnip and radish seeds just received from London; a dacha with all its land, including two horse boxes and an area where you could lay out an excellent birch or fir plantation; then there was a call to anyone wishing to buy old shoe soles, with an invitation to come trading every day between eight and three o'clock. The room in which all these people were was small and extremely stuffy, but Collegiate Assessor Kovalyov could not distinguish any smell, because he kept his face covered with a handkerchief and because the nose itself was God knows where.

"Dear sir, may I ask you... I really need to be seen," Kovalyov said, losing patience at last.

"Right away, right away! Two roubles forty-three copecks! This minute! One rouble sixty four copecks!" said the grey-haired gentleman, flinging the notices at the old women and caretakers. "What do you want?" he said at last, turning to Kovalyov.

"I'm asking..." Kovalyov said. "At this point I've no idea whether it was trickery or a swindle. I just want to advertise that whoever brings me that scoundrel will get a suitable reward."

"Could you please give me your surname?"

"No – why my surname? I won't give it. I have many acquaintances: Chekhtareva, a State Councillor's wife, Palageya Grigorevna Podtochina, a Staff Officer's wife... God forbid they should suddenly find out! You can simply write down Collegiate Assessor or, even better, one holding the rank of Major."

"Was the runaway your house serf?"

"What house serf? That wouldn't be such treachery! The runaway is… my nose…"

"Hm! What a strange surname! And did Mr Nosov steal a great deal from you?"

"Nose, I said… You've misunderstood me! My nose, my very own nose has disappeared who knows where. The Devil wanted to play a trick on me!"

"In what way did it disappear? There's something I don't quite understand."

"I myself can't tell you how it happened, but the main thing is that he drives around town and calls himself a state councillor. Which is why I ask you to advertise that anyone who catches him should speedily bring him to me at the earliest opportunity. Judge for yourself: how can I go on without such a conspicuous part of my body? It's not the same as some little toe which I put in a boot and whose absence no one will notice. On Thursdays I visit Chekhtareva, the State Councillor's wife; Palageya Grigorevna Podtochina, the Staff Officer's wife and her daughter, a very pretty girl, are also close friends, and now just think, how can I… I can't possibly show myself there now…"

The clerk's tightly pressed lips indicated that he was mulling this over.

"No, I can't place such a notice in the papers," he said at last after a long silence.

"How? Why?"

"The paper could lose its reputation. If everyone started writing that his nose had run away, then… As it is, people are already saying that we print a lot of absurd things and false rumours."

"What's absurd about this case? It's nothing like that."

"You may not think so. This is what happened last week: a civil servant came here the same way you did, brought a notice, the cost of which came to two roubles seventy-three copecks, and the notice only stated that a black-haired poodle had run away. You'd think nothing of it? But it turned out to be slander: that poodle was no other than the bursar of I don't remember what institution."

"I'm not giving you a notice about a poodle, but about my very own nose: it's almost the same as if it were about myself."

"No, there's no way I can place such an advertisement."

"Even though my nose really has disappeared?"

"If it has disappeared, then it's a medical case. They say that there are people who can fit you with any kind of nose. However, I notice that you seem to be a man of cheerful disposition and enjoy a joke in company."

"I swear to you by all that's holy! Please, even if it means my showing you."

"Why make such a fuss!" the clerk went on, taking a pinch of snuff. "On the other hand, if it doesn't disturb you," he added, stirred by curiosity, "then I'd like to have a look."

The Collegiate Assessor removed the handkerchief from his face.

"Indeed, it's extremely odd!" said the clerk. "The area is completely smooth, just like a freshly cooked pancake. It's unbelievably flat!"

"So, will you argue now? You can see for yourself that it's impossible not to advertise. I'd be particularly grateful, and I'm very pleased that this incident has given me the opportunity of making your acquaintance..."

As can be deduced from the above, the Major had decided to ingratiate himself a little.

"Printing this is of course a minor matter," said the clerk, "but I can't see how it can help you in any way? If you wish you could pass it on to someone who has a talent for writing, who could describe this as a rare natural phenomenon and publish the article in *The Northern Bee*"* – here he took some more snuff – "for the benefit of our young people" – here he wiped his nose – "or just for general interest."

The Collegiate Assessor felt completely abashed. He looked down at the lower section of the newspaper that announced theatrical performances. He was about to smile at seeing the name of a very pretty actress, and his hand sought his pocket to see whether it held a five-rouble banknote, because staff officers, in Kovalyov's opinion, should sit in the stalls – but the thought of the nose spoilt everything!

The clerk himself appeared to be moved by Kovalyov's plight. Trying somewhat to ease his distress, he deemed it proper to express his sympathy in a few words:

"I find it of course very regrettable that you've ended up in such a pickle. Would you care for a pinch of snuff? It squashes headaches and depression; it's even good for haemorrhoids."

With these words the clerk offered Kovalyov his snuffbox, quite nimbly lifting its lid portraying some lady with a hat.

This unmindful action exasperated Kovalyov.

"I don't understand how you can find time for jokes," he said angrily. "Can't you see that I don't have that with which to sniff? Damn your snuff! I can't bear to look at it, not only at that nasty Berezinsky snuff* of yours, but not even if you'd offered me *rapé* itself."

Having said this, he left the newspaper office deeply vexed and went to see the District Police Superintendent, who was a great lover of sugar. In his house, the whole of the hall, which also served as a dining room, was packed with sugar loaves, brought to him by merchants as tokens of friendship. The cook was at that moment pulling off the District Superintendent's official jackboots; his sword and all his military trappings were hanging peacefully in various corners of the room, and his three-year-old son was already fondling his formidable three-cornered hat; and he, after his fighting, martial life, was getting ready to taste the pleasures of peace.

Kovalyov arrived just as he gave a good stretch, grunted and said: "Ah, I'll have a good nap for an hour or two!" And so you could foresee that the arrival of the Collegiate Assessor was very untimely, and I'm not sure whether Kovalyov would have been any better received had he brought him a few pounds of tea or some cloth. The Superintendent was a great promoter of all the arts and manufactured goods, but he loved a banknote best of all. "That really is something," he would say, "and there's nothing to beat it: it doesn't require food, takes little room, always fits in a pocket and if you drop it, it doesn't break."

The Superintendent received Kovalyov rather stiffly and said that after dinner was not the time to carry out investigations, that nature itself prescribed a period of rest after a hearty meal (this made the Collegiate Assessor realize that the Superintendent was very much au fait with the maxims of ancient sages), that noses are not torn off respectable men, and that there are lots of majors of all sorts around who do not even own decent underwear and hang about in all kinds of tawdry places.

In other words, he struck home! It must be said that Kovalyov was extremely touchy. He could excuse anything that was said about his own person, but he never condoned anything that had to do with his rank or title. He even believed that in the theatre you could allow any reference to chief officers, but that you should never attack staff officers. The Superintendent's reception threw him into such a state of confusion that he shook his head and, spreading his arms out a little, said with dignity: "I must say that I have nothing to add after those offensive remarks of yours..." and left.

He returned home, scarcely able to feel his legs under him. It was already dusk. After all that fruitless searching the apartment felt sombre and extremely squalid. As he entered the front room, he caught sight of Ivan, his valet, who was lying on his back on the scruffy leather sofa, repeatedly spitting up at the ceiling and hitting the same spot rather successfully. Such disregard infuriated him; he whacked him across the forehead with his hat, saying: "You're always up to something stupid, you swine!"

Ivan promptly jumped up and rushed over to remove his cloak.

Once in his room, the Major, tired and despondent, threw himself into an armchair and, at last, after some deep sighing, said:

"My God, my God! Why such misfortune! Were I without arms or legs, it would have been better than this; were I without ears, that would have been bad, but still bearable – but a man without a nose, what on earth is that? He's not a bird, not a citizen; you might as well swing him out of the window! Had it been chopped off in battle or in a duel, or had I been responsible for it myself... but it just went missing for no reason at all, pointlessly! But no, it can't be," he added, pausing for thought. "It's inconceivable that a nose should go missing, it's just not possible. It's either a dream or a product of the imagination. It's possible that, instead of water, I mistakenly drank the vodka with which I rub my chin after shaving. That fool Ivan didn't take it away and I probably grabbed it."

To satisfy himself that he really was not drunk, he pinched himself so hard that he cried out in pain. This completely convinced him that he was fully functional and awake. He slowly drew near to the mirror and began by screwing up his eyes, with the thought that, just maybe, his nose would appear in its rightful place, but at the same moment he recoiled with the words:

"What a scandalous sight!"

It was indeed baffling. Had it been a button, a silver spoon, a watch or something similar that had gone missing... But for such a thing as a nose to go missing? And to top it all, in your own apartment! Major Kovalyov, looking at it from all angles, surmised that the blame lay most likely with Podtochina, the Staff Officer's wife, who wanted him to marry her daughter. He himself had enjoyed flirting with her, but had avoided a decisive confrontation. When the Staff Officer's wife had declared outright that she wanted to give her daughter in marriage to him, he had gradually eased up on his compliments, saying that he was still young and needed to be in service for about five years before turning forty-two. Which was why the Staff Officer's wife, probably in revenge, had decided to maim him and had hired some witches for this purpose, because there was no reason whatsoever to suppose that the nose had been cut off: no one had come into his room; the barber Ivan Yakovlevich had shaved him on Wednesday, and the rest of that day, as well as the whole of Thursday, his nose had been intact – he did remember and knew this for a fact. Besides, he would have felt some pain, and the wound could definitely not have healed that fast and be as smooth as a pancake. He worked out some plans in his head: should he officially have the Staff Officer's wife summoned in court or should he come to her in person and expose her. His reflections were interrupted by the light shining through the door chinks, which announced that the candle in the front room had already been lit by Ivan. Soon Ivan himself showed up, carrying the candle in front of him and brightly lighting up the whole room. Kovalyov's first impulse was to grab the handkerchief and cover the place where his nose had been the day before, to avoid the fool gaping at him at the sight of his master's odd appearance.

No sooner had Ivan gone to his cubbyhole than an unfamiliar voice was heard in the hall, saying:

"Does Collegiate Assessor Kovalyov live here?"

"Do come in. Major Kovalyov is in," Kovalyov said, hurriedly jumping up and opening the door.

A handsome police officer came in, with whiskers that were neither too dark nor too fair and with rather rounded cheeks, the very same one who, at the beginning of the story, had stood at the end of St Isaac's Bridge.

"Did you happen to mislay your nose?"

"I did indeed."

"It has now been found."

"What's that you're saying?" shouted Major Kovalyov. Joy left him speechless. He kept his eyes rooted to the police officer standing before him, whose full lips and cheeks gleamed in the flickering candlelight. "How did it happen?"

"By a strange coincidence: he was intercepted virtually on the road. He had already taken a seat on a stagecoach and wanted to go to Riga. And his passport was registered in the name of some official. And the strange thing is that I initially did take him for a gentleman. But fortunately I had my glasses with me and saw straight away that he was a nose. You see, I'm short-sighted, and if you're close to me then I can only see that you have a face, but I can't make out your nose or beard or anything else. My mother-in-law – my wife's mother that is – can't see anything either."

Kovalyov was beside himself.

"Where is he? Where? I'll go there straight away."

"Don't worry. Knowing that you would need him, I brought him with me. And the odd thing is that the main accomplice in this affair is that rogue, the barber of Vosnesensky Street, who is sitting right now in the police station. I've long suspected him of drunkenness and thieving, and even three days ago he walked off with a dozen buttons from a stall. Your nose is exactly as it was before."

With this the police officer reached into his pocket and pulled out the nose wrapped in paper.

"That's it!" exclaimed Kovalyov. "That is it indeed! Do join me today for a cup of tea."

"I would consider it a great pleasure, but I really can't. I have to call in at the mental institution... The costs of all goods has risen sharply... At home I have living with me my mother-in-law – that is, my wife's mother – and my children. The eldest shows great promise – he's a very clever boy, but I just don't have the means to educate him..."

Kovalyov guessed what he was after and, grabbing a ten-rouble note from the table, thrust it into the hand of the inspector who, clicking his heels, went out the door, and in almost the same instant Kovalyov heard his voice in the street reprimanding, together with a punch to the teeth, some stupid muzhik who had driven his cart right onto the boulevard.

After the police officer's departure the Collegiate Assessor remained in a state of uncertainty for a few moments, and it was only several minutes later that he was able to see or feel anything, so completely overcome was he by the unexpected joy. He carefully took the newly found nose in his cupped hands and once again inspected it attentively.

"That's really it!" Major Kovalyov said. "There on the left is the pimple that popped up yesterday."

The Major almost burst out laughing with joy.

But nothing lasts long in this world, and so the joy felt in the instant following that first one is already less keen: it palls even further in the third minute, and in the end it imperceptibly blends in with your usual mood, just like a ring formed from a pebble falling in the water finally blends in with the water's smooth surface. Kovalyov began to mull things over and realized that the affair was not over yet. The nose was found, but it still had to be positioned in its usual place.

"And what if it won't stay on?"

At posing himself such a question, the Major turned pale.

He rushed to the table with a feeling of indescribable terror and moved the mirror to avoid attaching the nose somehow lopsidedly. His hands trembled. He placed it carefully and deliberately in its former place. Oh, horrors! The nose would not stick! He brought it to his lips and warmed it lightly with his breath, then again placed it on the smooth area in between the two cheeks, but the nose would just not stay on.

"Now, come on! Stay on, you fool!" he kept on saying. But the nose seemed to be made of wood and dropped on the table with a strange, cork-like sound. The Major's face twisted convulsively. "Couldn't it grow back?" he muttered terrified. But however many times he placed the nose where it belonged, he was always unsuccessful.

He called Ivan and sent him for the doctor, who occupied the best apartment in the same building, on the first floor. The doctor was a fine figure of a man; he had beautiful pitch-black side whiskers, a fresh and healthy young wife, ate fresh apples in the morning and kept his mouth exceptionally clean, rinsing it for nearly three quarters of an hour every morning, scrubbing his teeth with five different kinds of brushes. The doctor appeared promptly. He asked how long ago the accident had happened and then lifted Major Kovalyov's face by the chin and flicked him with his thumb on the very spot where the nose had been, which made the Major throw his head backwards with such force that he hit the back of his head against the wall. The doctor said that it was nothing and suggested he move away from the wall a little, told him to bend his head first to the right and, having fingered that place where the nose had been before, said: "Hm!" Then he told him to bend his head to the left and said: "Hm!" and finally flicked him again with his thumb, which made Major Kovalyov jerk his head like a horse having its teeth inspected. After this examination, the doctor shook his head and said:

"No, it's impossible. You'd better just stay as you are, because we could make matters worse. It can of course be fixed – I can fix it right away – but I assure you that it would be worse for you."

"That's a good one! How am I to remain without a nose?"
Kovalyov said. "It can't be worse than it already is. What the
hell is this? Where can I show myself with such a monstros-
ity? I have well-connected acquaintances. This very evening
I'm expected at soirées in two different homes. I know many
people: Chekhtareva, a State Councillor's wife, Podtochina, a
Staff Officer's wife, although after her latest exploit I'm having
nothing more to do with her, except through the police. Do me
a favour," pleaded Kovalyov, "is there no way? Fix it somehow;
it may not be perfect, but as long as it stays on... I could even
prop it up with my hand in dangerous situations. I don't dance
anyway, so there's no risk of a careless movement harming it.
As regards my gratitude for the consultation, rest assured that
as far as my means permit—"

"Believe me when I say," the doctor said, not loudly or softly
but in an exceptionally affable and persuasive voice, "that I
never give treatment for profit. It goes against my principles
and my art. True, I take something for consultations, but only
to avoid offending by refusing. I would of course fix your nose
back on, but I assure you, on my honour, if my word is not
sufficient for you, that it will make matters much worse. Better
let nature take its course. Wash more often with cold water and
I assure you that you'll be as healthy without a nose as with
one. And I advise you to put the nose in a jar with alcohol or,
even better, add two tablespoons of strong preservative and

heated vinegar and you could get good money for it. I'll take it myself if you don't charge too much."

"No, no! I won't sell it for anything!" yelled Major Kovalyov in desperation. "Let it go to the Devil instead!"

"Excuse me!" said the doctor, taking his leave. "I wanted to help you…Too bad! At least you've seen me try."

Having said this, the doctor left the room with a lofty air. Kovalyov did not even notice his face and, in his dazed state, could only make out the cuffs of his shirt, clean and white as snow, peeping out from the sleeves of his black tailcoat.

He made a decision the very next day, before filing a complaint, to write to the Staff Officer's wife, asking whether she would agree to return to him, without a fight, what was his due. The content of the letter was as follows:

Dear Madam,

Alexandra Grigoryevna!

I am unable to understand your strange conduct. Rest assured that you will gain nothing by acting in this way and that you certainly cannot force me to marry your daughter. Believe me when I tell you that I am in full knowledge of the affair of my nose and the fact that you and no one else are its main instigator. The sudden disconnection from its place, its flight and its taking on, at first, the guise of a civil servant before finally changing back to its usual form is nothing else than the result of witchcraft initiated by you or by those who, like you, practise those noble pursuits. For my part I regard it as my duty to warn you: if the above-mentioned nose is not returned to its rightful place by today, I shall be compelled to turn to the defence and the protection of the law.

I am, respectfully yours,

Your humble servant,

Platon Kovalyov

Dear Sir,

Platon Kuzmich!

I found your letter extremely surprising. I'll honestly confess that I didn't expect it, particularly as regards the unjust reproaches on your part. I warn you that I have never received the civil servant of whom you speak, whether masked or otherwise in my home. Filipp Ivanovich Potanchikov used to call at my house, it's true. And although he did indeed seek my daughter's hand, being a good, sober and highly educated man, I never gave him any reason for hope. You also mention a nose. If you mean by it that I was turning my nose up at you, in other words giving you a formal refusal, then I'm amazed that you are the one to mention it, when you know that I'm of a completely different opinion, and if you now seek my daughter's hand lawfully I am prepared to agree immediately, as it has always been

my keenest wish, and in the hope of which I remain ever
your humble servant,

Alexandra Podtochina

"No." said Kovalyov after reading the letter. "She's definitely not guilty. It's impossible. A person who is guilty of a crime can't possibly write a letter like that." Collegiate Assessor Kovalyov was an expert in these matters, because he had been sent on a few investigations when still in the Caucasus. "How in the world has this happened? Only the Devil can make sense of it all!" he said at last, letting his arms drop.

Meanwhile rumours of this extraordinary incident had spread throughout the capital and, as usual, not without additional embellishment. At the time everyone's mind was particularly susceptible to the paranormal: the public had just recently shown interest in experiments in magnetism. Besides, the story of the dancing chairs in Konyushennaya Street was still fresh in people's minds, which is why it was no surprise when people soon began saying that Collegiate Assessor Kovalyov's nose was in the habit of strolling along Nevsky Prospect at exactly three o'clock. Many gathered there every day out of curiosity. Someone said that the nose was to be found in Junker's Store* – and there was such a crowd and a crush near Junker's that even the police had to intervene. One speculator of respectable appearance, with side whiskers, who sold a variety of dry pastries by the theatre entrance, purposely produced some lovely solid wooden benches on which he invited the curious to stand for eighty copecks per person. One distinguished Colonel left home early for that very purpose, and made his way through the crowd with great difficulty; but, much to his indignation, all he saw in the shop window, instead of a nose, was an ordinary woollen sweater and a lithograph depicting a young girl adjusting her stocking while a dandy with a lapelled waistcoat and a small beard was taking a peek at her from behind a tree – a picture that had hung in the same spot for over ten years. He moved away and said crossly: "How can they mislead people with such ridiculous and improbable rumours?"

Then the rumour spread that Major Kovalyov's nose did not go strolling on Nevsky Prospect but in Tauride Garden,* and that it had been there all along; also that when Khozrev-Mirza* had stayed there he had been greatly startled by such a strange trick of nature. Some students from the College of Surgeons made their way there. One excellent, respectable lady put in a request by special letter to the garden supervisor to show her children this rare phenomenon, if possible with an explanation that would be edifying and instructive for the young.

Particularly pleased with these incidents were all those society men, essential guests at evening receptions, who loved to make ladies laugh, and whose stock had completely run out at the time. A small number of respectable and well-meaning people were extremely displeased. One gentleman stated indignantly that he couldn't understand how in this enlightened age such absurd stories could be circulated, and that he was surprised that the government didn't look into the matter. That gentleman, it's obvious, belonged to those who wanted the government to be involved in everything, even in his daily arguments with his wife. After this... but at this point the whole incident is once again completely shrouded in mist, and what came next is definitely not known.

3

THE MOST NONSENSICAL things go on in this world. Sometimes it's beyond belief: that very nose, which had driven around as a state councillor and had caused such a stir in town, ended up all of a sudden, as though nothing had happened, in its rightful place, namely between Major Kovalyov's two cheeks. It happened on 7th April. When he woke up and inadvertently glanced in the mirror he saw... his nose! He grabbed it with his hand – it was his nose indeed! "Aha!" Kovalyov said, and in his joy he almost burst into a *trepak** barefoot all across the room, but was disturbed by the arrival of Ivan. He immediately asked for water and soap, and while he washed he again peeped in the mirror: his nose! As he dried himself with the towel he looked again: his nose!

"Look, Ivan, there appears to be a pimple on my nose," he said, meanwhile thinking: "What a disaster if Ivan says: 'No, sir, not only is there no pimple, but there's no nose either!'"

But Ivan said:

"There isn't a pimple at all: your nose is spotless."

"That's good, damn it!" the Major said to himself, snapping his fingers. At that moment Ivan Yakovlevich, the barber, looked in at the door, but as warily as a cat who has just been whipped for stealing lard.

"Tell me first of all: are your hands clean?" Kovalyov yelled at him from a distance.

"They're clean."

"You're a liar!"

"They're clean, sir, honestly."

"Well, look out."

Kovalyov sat down. Ivan Yakovlevich covered him with a napkin and, with the help of his brush, transformed the entire beard and part of the cheeks in no time into the kind of cream that is served on merchants' name days.

"Well I never!" Ivan Yakovlevich said to himself after glancing at the nose, and then he tilted Kovalyov's head the other way and looked at it sideways. "Look at that! How can you figure it out?" he went on and stared at the nose for a long time. At last, ever so gently, taking as much care as you could only imagine, he raised two fingers in order to take hold of it by the tip. That was Ivan Yakovlevich's method.

"Now do be careful!" Kovalyov cried out.

Overcome and more confused than he had ever been before, Ivan Yakovlevich let his hands drop. He finally began to tickle Kovalyov carefully with his razor under the chin and, although it was rather awkward and difficult for him to shave without holding on to the olfactory part of the body, by somehow pressing his gnarled thumb against the cheek and the lower jaw, he at last overcame all obstacles and shaved him.

When it was all done, Kovalyov hurried to get dressed at once, called for a carriage and went straight to the patisserie. Barely inside, he called out: "Boy, a hot chocolate!" at the same time glancing in the mirror: the nose was there! He turned round happily and, with a sarcastic look, watched, slightly screwing up his eyes, two military men, one of whom had a nose no bigger than a waistcoat button. After that he went to the office of the department where he was soliciting for the post of vice-governor and, failing that, of procurement officer. As he walked through the front hall he glanced at the mirror: the nose was there! Then he went over to see another Collegiate Assessor, or Major, a great joker to whom he often said in reply to various abrasive remarks: "Oh, come now, I know you, you're a tease!" On the way there he thought: "If even the Major doesn't collapse with laughter when he sees me, then that's a sure sign that absolutely everything is in its proper place." But the Collegiate Assessor made no comment. "That's good, damn it!" Kovalyov thought to himself. On the way he met Podtochina, the Staff Officer's wife, together with her daughter, exchanged bows and was met with joyful outpourings: there clearly was no fallout whatsoever. He spent a very long time chatting with them and deliberately took out his snuffbox, stuffed his nose in front of them for quite a long time using both holes, muttering to himself: "There's to you, you stupid hens! And I still won't marry the daughter! Simply *par amour*, if you please!" And from then on Major Kovalyov would saunter as though nothing had happened along Nevsky Prospect, to the theatre and just about everywhere. And his nose too sat on his face as though nothing had happened, not giving the slightest indication that it had absented itself. And after that Major Kovalyov was always to be seen in a good mood, smiling, resolutely pursuing all pretty women and even once stopping at a counter in Gostiny Dvor* and buying some medal ribbon, for reasons unknown, as he was not the bearer of any decoration.

So that's the incident that happened in the northern capital of our vast nation! Only now, on all accounts, do we see that there's much that is improbable here. Even without mentioning the truly supernatural severing of the nose and its appearance in various locations in the guise of a civil servant – had it not occurred to Kovalyov that it was just not done to put out a notice about a nose via a newspaper office? I don't mean in the sense of it being an expensive thing to advertise – that's nonsense and I'm not mercenary at all. But it is unseemly, awkward, wrong! And then again – how did the nose end up in a bread loaf and how did Ivan Yakovlevich... No, I really don't understand, I absolutely do not understand! But, stranger still, what is quite incomprehensible is how authors can choose such subjects. I admit, it's inconceivable, it's simply... no, I just don't understand it. Firstly, it's of no use whatsoever to our fatherland, and secondly... secondly there's no use here either. I just don't know what it's all about...

Yet, with all that, though you could allow for this or that or the other, maybe even... after all, where do absurd situations not occur? Yet, when you think about it, there's something in it. Whatever anyone says, such things do happen in this world – rarely, but they do happen.

The Overcoat

I N THE DEPARTMENT OF... no, it's better not to name the department. There's nothing more touchy than departments, regiments or offices of all kinds – in short, official bodies of all kinds. These days every private individual considers the whole of society to be insulted when he is. They say that quite recently a petition was received from a certain chief of police from I don't remember which town, in which he clearly states that government decrees are falling apart and that his own sacred name is definitely being uttered in vain. To prove this he appended to his petition a huge volume of some romantic novel, in which a chief of police features every ten pages, even here and there in a completely inebriated state. And so, to avoid any kind of unpleasantness, it's best we refer to the department in question as *a certain department*. So, in *a certain department* there worked *a certain clerk*. It could not be said that this clerk stood out in any way: he was shortish, somewhat pockmarked, somewhat ginger-haired, even somewhat short-sighted, with a small bald patch in front, wrinkles on both his cheeks and what we would call a haemorrhoidal complexion... It can't be helped! The Petersburg climate is to blame. As for his rank (for we must first of all announce his rank), he was what is known as an eternal titular councillor, one of those who, as we know, have been abundantly mocked and joked about by several writers who have the commendable habit of attacking those who cannot bite back. The clerk's surname was Bashmachkin. The very name suggests that at some point in time it derived from the word *bashmak* or "shoe", but when or at what time and how it had derived from *bashmak* is totally unknown. His father and grandfather, and even his brother-in-law and every single Bashmachkin in fact, went around in boots which they had resoled only three times a year. His name was Akaky Akakievich. Perhaps the reader may find it a bit strange and contrived, but rest assured that it was not contrived at all, and that such circumstances came about which made it impossible to give him any other name, and here's exactly how it happened. Akaky Akakievich was born, if my memory serves me right, as night fell on 23rd March. His late mother, the wife of a civil servant and a very good woman, duly made arrangements to have the child christened. The mother was still lying on her bed opposite the door, and on her right stood the godfather, Ivan Ivanovich Yeroshkin, a most excellent man who served as a senior clerk in the Senate, and the godmother, Anna Semyonovna Belobriushkova, a police inspector's wife and a woman of rare virtue. They offered a choice of three names to the new baby's mother: Mokkiya, Sossiya or – to name the child after a martyr – Khozdazat.* "No," thought the late mother. "What awful names we keep on getting." To please her, they went to another calendar* entry and again three names came up: Trifily, Dula and Varakhasy. "Well, that's a proper cross to bear," the old girl said. "What names they all are: I've truly never heard the like. Varadat or even Varykh might do well enough, but not Trifily or Varakhasy." They turned another page and up came Pavsikakhy and Vakhtisy. "Now I see," the old girl said. "It's obviously his destiny. If that's so, then he'd better be named after his father. His father was Akaky, so let the son also be Akaky." That was how he came to be Akaky Akakievich. The baby was christened, during which ceremony he started crying and pulled such a face as though he sensed that he would become a titular councillor. So that's how it all came to be. We've pointed this out so that the reader could see for himself that it all came about purely out of necessity, and to have given Akaky any other name would have been absolutely impossible. When precisely he started working in the department and who appointed him, no one could remember. However many directors and department heads came and went, he was always to be seen at the same spot, in the same position, holding the same job as the same copying clerk – so that later they were convinced that he must have been born like that, complete in his uniform and with a bald patch on his head. He was shown no respect at all within the department. Not only did the porters fail to get up when he walked past, but they did not even give him a glance, as though a common fly had flitted across the waiting room. The Department Heads behaved rather coldly and despotically towards him. Some senior clerk's aide would simply shove documents under his nose without even saying "copy those", or "here's a nice, interesting little job", or some nicety as is customary in a refined office environment. And he would take the document, looking only at the paper and not glancing up at the person who had put it there or checking whether that person had the right to do so. He took it and immediately set to copying it. The young clerks laughed at him and made jokes about him, to the extent that office wit would allow, and in his presence told various made-up stories about him; they said that his landlady, a seventy-year-old woman, beat him, they asked when the wedding would be and scattered bits of paper over his head, calling it snow. But Akaky Akakievich did not respond to any of this, as though there was nobody at all before him. It did not even influence his work: in the face of all this aggravation he did not make one single mistake in his writing. Only if the joke became just too unbearable, when they nudged his arm and prevented him from doing his work, would he say: "Leave me alone, why do you insult me?" And there was something strange in the words as well as in the voice with which he pronounced them. You could hear something that inclined you to pity, so much so that one young man, who had not long been appointed, and who, following the others' example, was about to join in the laughter, suddenly stopped short as though transfixed, and from that moment on everything seemed to change for him and look different. Some strange power pushed him away from those with whom he had become acquainted, having taken them to be respectable, cultured men. And long afterwards, in the middle of the most cheerful moments, he would be confronted with that short little clerk with the bald patch in front and the piercing words: "Leave me alone, why do you insult me?" – and together with those piercing words rang the sound of other words: "I'm your brother". And the poor young man would bury his face in his hands and shudder many times during his lifetime when he saw how much inhumanity there is in man, how much brutal crassness lies concealed within a refined, cultured gentility and even, oh God, in a man whom society regards as noble and upright...

You would be hard put to find a man who lived so much for his work. It is not enough to say he worked with zeal – no, he worked with love. There, in the copying, he saw a varied and pleasant world all his own. His face expressed delight; some letters were his favourites, and if he came across them he would be beside himself. He would laugh gently to himself and wink and use his lips to assist him, so that it seemed that you could read on his face every letter his pen was tracing. Had they given him rewards in keeping with his zeal he might, to his own surprise, perhaps even have reached the rank of state councillor. But, as those sharp-witted colleagues of his put it, in return for a badge in his buttonhole he got piles on his backside. Besides, you could not say that he was completely ignored. One director, being a kindly man and wanting to reward him for his long service, ordered that he should be given something rather more important than the usual copying job. He was asked to adapt an already existing document into some report for another government office: all he had to do was change the title and also change some verbs from the first person to the third person. This took so much effort out of him that he broke out in a complete sweat, kept wiping his forehead and in the end said: "No, you'd better just give me something to copy." From then on they left him to copy for good. Nothing seemed to exist for him beyond this copying. He gave no thought at all to his clothes: his uniform was not green, but of some mealy reddish colour. Its collar was very narrow and small, so that his neck, which was actually not very long, appeared unusually long as it stuck out of the collar, like those plaster kittens with waggling heads which foreign pedlars in Russia carry by the dozen on their heads. And something was always bound to cling to his uniform coat: either a sprig of hay or a strand of thread. And then he had the particular knack, as he walked along the street, to land under a window at the very moment when all sorts of rubbish were being thrown out, and so he always carried around strips of watermelon or other melon peel and similar litter on his hat. Not once in his life did he pay attention to what was going on in the street every day, whereas his young fellow clerk, as we know, is always on the lookout as he strains his sharp bold gaze far enough to notice even on the opposite pavement whose trouser strap has ripped below the trousers – something which always brings a mischievous grin to his face.

Yet if Akaky Akakievich did actually look at anything, he would see in everything his own neat lines written in his even script, unless, appearing from goodness knows where, a horse's head happened to settle on his shoulder blowing gusts of wind from its nostrils onto his cheek – only then would he notice that he was not in the middle of a line but rather in the middle of the street. After arriving home he would immediately sit down at the table, quickly gulp down his cabbage soup and eat a piece of beef and onion without taking any notice of its taste, and eat it all up, including flies or whatever else God might send his way. When he noticed his stomach beginning to bulge, he would get up from the table, take out the ink jar and copy out those documents he had brought home. If he had no work, then he would make a special copy for his own pleasure, particularly if the document stood out – not because of the beauty of its style, but because it was addressed to some new or important person.

Even in those hours when the grey St Petersburg sky completely fades away and all the civil-service folk have eaten their fill and finished dinner – each one in keeping with his salary and his own fancy – when rest has come to all and everything after the departmental scratching of quills, the running around, the performance of your own as well as others' necessary tasks, everything the unflinching person freely takes on, even beyond what is required – when clerks hurry off to devote the time that is left to pleasure: the bolder ones taking themselves to the theatre; others using their time on the lookout for some ladies' hats; others to go off to a party, to spend their time complimenting some pretty young girl, the star of a small civil-servant circle; others, and this happens most often, simply to go to visit their fellow clerk who lives on the fourth or third floor, in two small rooms with either a hall or a kitchen and some fashionable pretentious objects, a lamp or some small trinket, tokens of many sacrifices, with dinner or outing invitations refused – in a word, even at the time when all civil servants disperse to their friends' small apartments to play whist, sipping tea from glasses and eating dry biscuits, drawing smoke from long-stemmed pipes and, while dealing cards, airing some gossip gleaned from high society, something a Russian can never under any circumstances walk away from even when there is nothing to talk about, retelling the eternal joke about the garrison commandant who was told that a piece of the horse's tail had been cut off Falconet's statue* – in a word, even when there is a general urge to relax – Akaky Akakievich did not indulge in any form of relaxation. No one could say that he had ever been seen at any party. After writing to his heart's content, he went to bed, smiling already at the thought of the following day: what would he be given to copy tomorrow? So passed the peaceful life of a man who with a salary of a thousand was able to be happy with his lot, and it would perhaps have continued this way into ripe old age, were it not for various calamities scattered along the path of life not only of titular but even of privy, court and all kinds of councillors – even those who give no counsel to anyone nor take it from anyone themselves.

There is in St Petersburg a forceful enemy of anyone who earns four hundred roubles a year or as near a figure as that. This enemy is none other than our northern frost, although people do say it's very good for the health. Between eight and nine o'clock in the morning, at that very hour when the streets become filled with those making their way to the office, it begins to deal out indiscriminately such strong, sharp nips to everyone's nose that the poor clerks really do not know where to put themselves. At that time when even those who occupy high positions have foreheads aching from the frost and tears springing up in their eyes, the poor titular councillors are sometimes left defenceless. Their only salvation lies in running as fast as possible in their very thin little overcoats across five to six streets and then have a good stamp of their feet in the porter's lodge until all those faculties and assets, frozen on the way, thaw out completely and are ready for service. Akaky Akakievich had for a while begun to feel his back and shoulders particularly under attack, even though he tried to run as fast as he could along the designated route. In the end he wondered whether perhaps his overcoat was at fault here. Giving it a good inspection at home, he discovered that in two or three places, namely on the shoulders and on the back, it had become just like thin gauze; the cloth was so worn that it was transparent and the lining had disintegrated. It has to be said that Akaky Akakievich's overcoat had also been an object of ridicule with the clerks; they had even taken away its noble name of overcoat and called it a "dressing gown". It did indeed have a strange shape: its collar had grown smaller and smaller with every year of it being used to patch up other parts. This patching showed no signs of a tailor's expertise and looked slack and unsightly. Having sized up the situation, Akaky Akakievich decided that the coat should be taken to Petrovich the tailor, who lived somewhere on a fourth floor along a dark back staircase, and who, despite a dud eye and pockmarks all across his face, worked quite successfully, mending trousers and frock coats for civil servants and all sorts of other people – when he was sober, that is, and had no other projects in mind. There would of course be no reason to discuss this tailor at any length, but as it's accepted that each character of a story should be fully drawn, it can't be helped: let's have Petrovich. At first he was simply called Grigory and he was some landlord's serf. He began to be called Petrovich when he was granted his freedom and started to drink very heavily on feast days, at first only on the major ones, but then indiscriminately on all saints' days, whenever there was a small cross in the calendar. In this respect he was true to his ancestors' customs, and when he quarrelled with his wife he called her a worldly woman and a German. As we've now mentioned the wife, we'll have to say a word or two about her, but unfortunately little was known about her, except perhaps that Petrovich had a wife and that she actually wore a bonnet and not a headscarf. However, she could apparently not boast of being beautiful; at least, upon meeting her, only soldiers of the guards would take a look under her bonnet, twitching their moustaches and putting on a peculiar voice.

As he clambered up the staircase leading up to Petrovich's – and which, to give it its due, was smeared with water and slops and permeated with that smell of spirits which stings the eyes and, as we know, is always present in every back stairway of St Petersburg buildings – so, as he clambered up the staircase, Akaky Akakievich was already working out how much Petrovich would charge him and he mentally resolved not to give more than two roubles. The door was open, because the mistress of the house was cooking fish and had filled the kitchen with so much smoke that you could not even see the cockroaches. Akaky Akakievich stepped through the kitchen without even being spotted by the mistress of the house, and at last entered a room where he saw Petrovich, seated on a wide unpainted wooden table with his legs tucked under him like a Turkish pasha. His feet, as is usual with tailors sitting when at work, were bare. And the first thing that hit the eye was the big toe, very familiar to Akaky Akakievich, with a somewhat deformed toenail, thick and solid like a tortoise's shell. A skein of silk and threads hung around Petrovich's neck, and on his knees was some kind of rag. He had already been trying for about three minutes to thread the needle without success, and so had become very cross at the bad light, and even at the thread itself, grumbling under his breath: "Won't go in, the brute; you've worn me out, you rascal!" Akaky Akakievich did not like to come in just as Petrovich was cross: he preferred to order something from Petrovich when the latter was already under the influence or, as his wife expressed it, "when he's been swilling liquor, that one-eyed devil". In that condition, Petrovich was usually very eager to give way and to agree; he even bowed and thanked him each time. Then, it's true, the wife would come in, crying and saying that her husband was drunk and had therefore sold himself cheap; but then you would add a ten-copeck coin and the deal was in the bag. This time, it seemed, Petrovich was sober and hence abrupt, intractable and inclined to charge who knows what price. Akaky Akakievich picked up on this and was just about to make a run for it, as they say, but the first step had already been taken. Petrovich screwed up his one eye intently at him and Akaky Akakievich said helplessly:

"Good day, Petrovich!"

"And I wish you a good day, sir," said Petrovich, and he squinted with his one eye towards Akaky Akakievich's hands to see what kind of loot he had brought.

"Well, I'm here to see you, Petrovich, er..."

You should know that Akaky Akakievich expressed himself mostly with prepositions, adverbs and, in the end, such particles that decidedly hold no meaning at all. If it had to do with a very difficult matter, then he was in the habit of not finishing off his sentences at all, so that very often, having begun with the words: "It's, in truth, quite so er..." and with nothing to follow this, he himself would become forgetful, thinking that he had finished what he had to say.

"What's this?" Petrovich said, at the same time scrutinizing the entire uniform with his one eye, beginning with the collar, then the sleeves, back, tails and buttonholes – all of which was very familiar to him, as it had been his own work. Such is the tailor's habit: it's the first thing he does when he meets you.

"Well, I'm here er... Petrovich... the overcoat, the cloth... so, you see, it's quite sturdy everywhere, it just got a bit dusty, as though it's old, but it's quite new, it's just that one spot where it's a bit er... on the back, and just here by the shoulder it's a bit worn through, here also on this shoulder just a little – you see, that's all. Just a little work..."

Petrovich took the "dressing gown", laid it out first on the table, inspected it all over for a long time, shook his head and reached his hand out to the window sill for his round snuffbox with a portrait on it of some general – who, exactly, is not known, because his face had been poked through by a finger and then pasted over with a square scrap of paper. Having taken some snuff, Petrovich spread the dressing gown out with both hands and looked at it through the light and shook his head again. Then he turned the lining inside out and shook his head again, took off the lid with the general pasted with paper, filled his nose with snuff, shut the snuffbox, hid it away and at last said:

"No, it can't be mended: it's a thin garment!"

At those words Akaky Akakievich's heart missed a beat.

"Why not, Petrovich?" he said, almost in a child's plaintive voice. "It's just that it's only a bit worn thin on the shoulders – you must have some little pieces of cloth..."

"Oh yes, I can find some little pieces all right; little pieces will be found," said Petrovich, "but it's impossible to sew them on: it's just rotten, and if you touch it with a needle it'll simply fall to bits."

"Let it fall to bits, then you can mend it at once with a patch."

"But there's nowhere to place a patch, there's nothing to fix it to, just too much wear. It just calls itself cloth, but let the wind blow and it will scatter in the air."

"Well then, add more cloth. How can it be, really, er..."

"No," Petrovich said firmly. "There's nothing for it. It's in a very bad way. You'd better, as suits the winter cold, make some cloths out of it to wrap around your feet, because stockings are not warm. It's the Germans who invented them to make more money for themselves" – Petrovich liked on occasion to have a go at the Germans – "and you obviously need to have a new overcoat made."

At the word "new", Akaky Akakievich's eyes misted over and everything in the room became blurred. All he saw clearly was the general, with his face stuck over with a scrap of paper, on the lid of Petrovich's snuffbox.

"What do you mean, new?" he said, still feeling as though in a dream. "I just don't have the money for that."

"Yes, a new one," Petrovich said with brutal composure.

"Well, if I need a new one, how would, er..."

"Do you mean how much would it cost?"

"Yes."

"Well, you'd have to put by a bit over three fifties," Petrovich said, and with this he pressed his lips together meaningfully. He had a great liking for powerful effects, he loved to cause total bewilderment and would then cast a sidelong glance to see what the bewildered face looked like after such words.

"One hundred and fifty roubles for an overcoat!" poor Akaky Akakievich cried out, and perhaps it was the first time he had cried out in all his life, as he was always noted for his soft voice.

"Yes sir," Petrovich said, "and not much of an overcoat at that. If you were to add marten fur to the collar and stick on a hood with silk lining, it could even go up to two hundred."

"Petrovich, please," Akaky Akakievich implored, not hearing or even trying to hear Petrovich's words and those powerful effects of his. "Mend it somehow, so that it can be of some use still."

"No, it doesn't make sense: both wasted work and money spent for nothing." Petrovich said, and after such words Akaky Akakievich left the room totally crushed.

After his departure, Petrovich stood for a long time, pressing his lips together meaningfully without getting back to work, satisfied that he had neither let himself down nor betrayed the tailor's art.

Once on the street, Akaky Akakievich felt like he was dreaming. "What a business," he said to himself. "I really didn't think it would turn out, er..." – and then, after a brief silence he added: "What a thing! That's how it's turned out, and I really couldn't have imagined that it would be like this." Another long silence followed this, and then he said: "So it's like this! That's how it has come about, so unexpected, er... it can't... what a situation!" After those words, instead of going home he walked in completely the opposite direction without being aware of it. On the way, a chimney sweep brushed his whole dirty side against him and blackened his shoulder; an entire hatful of lime spilt all over him from the top of a house under construction. He did not notice a thing, and only later, when he bumped into a policeman who, having put his halberd aside, was busy shaking some snuff out of a snuff horn onto his calloused fist, did he recover his senses a little, and only because the policeman said to him: "What are you doing creeping right up to my ugly mug? Can't you stick to the pavement?" This made him look round and turn back in the direction of home. It was only there that he began to collect his thoughts, to see his situation in clear daylight, and he began to talk to himself no longer disconnectedly but soberly and openly, as with a sensible friend with whom you could discuss intimate matters closest to your heart. "No," Akaky Akakievich said, "it's impossible to discuss anything with Petrovich right now: he's now, er... his wife must have given him a beating. I'd do better to go to him on Sunday, in the morning: after the Saturday he'll be squinting and sleepy, he'll need another drink, but his wife won't give him the money, and at that moment I'll put a small ten-copeck coin, er... in his hand, and he'll be more tractable, and then the overcoat and er..." In this way did Akaky Akakievich reason with himself and cheer himself up, and he waited for the following Sunday and, seeing from a distance that Petrovich's wife had left the house on an errand somewhere, he walked straight over. Indeed, Petrovich, after the Saturday, was squinting hard: his head was drooping and he was very sleepy – but all the same, as soon as he realized what this was about, he seemed to be touched by the Devil. "It's impossible," he said. "Be so good as to order a new one." At that point Akaky Akakievich slipped him a ten-copeck coin. "I thank you, sir; I'll fortify myself a little with a drink to your health," said Petrovich, "and don't worry yourself about the overcoat: it's of no use to anyone. I'll make you a new overcoat myself, and a magnificent one at that – let's stick to that."

Akaky Akakievich tried to suggest mending it again, but Petrovich did not hear him out and said: "I'll definitely make you a new one, you may rely on it; we'll put in the effort. We may even make it in keeping with the latest style: the collar will be fastened with silver-plated clasps."

It was at this point that Akaky Akakievich saw that he could not do without a new overcoat, and his spirits sank completely. How, how indeed, with what, with what money could he have it made? He could of course partly count on a future holiday bonus, but that money had long ago been set aside and spoken for. He had to buy a new pair of trousers, pay the cobbler an old debt back for putting new toecaps on old boots, and he had to order three shirts from the seamstress and two items of that underwear which it is improper to refer to in print – in a word, all that money was to be spent. And even if the director were so well disposed as to grant him forty-five or fifty roubles in bonus payment instead of forty, he still would be left with a trifling amount, a drop in the ocean in terms of the capital needed for the overcoat. Although he knew, of course, that Petrovich could suddenly get carried away by a whim, quoting the Devil knows what exorbitant price, so that the wife herself would not be able to stop from crying out: "What, have you lost your mind, you fool! One moment he won't take in any work and now the Devil drives him to ask a price he's not worthy of himself." Although he knew, of course, that Petrovich would take the job on for eighty roubles, still, where could he get eighty roubles from? He might be able to find half that, half could be rustled up, maybe even a little over half, but where would the other half come from?... But the reader must first find out where that first half would come from. Akaky Akakievich was in the habit of setting aside half a copeck out of each rouble spent, and he would put it in a small locked box which had a little hole cut out on the top for dropping coins in. Every six months he inspected the saved-up coins and exchanged them for silver ones. That is what he had been doing for a very long time, and so in the course of several years it turned out that he had accumulated more than forty roubles. So he had half the money, but where to find the other half? Where to find another forty roubles? Akaky Akakievich thought and thought, and decided that he would have to reduce his usual expenses for at least a year: banish the use of tea in the evenings, not light the candle in the evenings, and if he had to do something, then go to the landlady's room and work by the light of her candle. When walking on the road, tread more lightly and carefully on its stones and slabs, almost on tiptoe, to avoid wearing out the soles too quickly; send his linen less frequently to the laundry and, to avoid it getting dirty from long wear, take it off every time he got home and just wear his cotton dressing gown, a very old one which even time itself had spared. It must be said that he initially found it hard to get used to such restrictions, but then he somehow got used to them and it all went well. He even accustomed himself to going without food in the evening, being spiritually fed instead, constantly carrying in his thoughts the idea of his future overcoat. From then on his existence seemed to become fuller, as though he had got married, as though another person were present alongside him, as though he was not alone and some nice female friend had agreed to walk the path of life together with him – and that friend was none other than that thickly quilted overcoat with a strong lining made to last. He became more lively somehow, even stronger in character, like a person who had already defined and established a purpose for himself. Self-doubt and indecisiveness – in short all those hesitations and vague traits – vanished from his face and actions. There were times when his eyes fired up and the most daring and valiant thoughts flashed through his mind: what about some marten fur on the collar perhaps? Thinking about it almost made him distracted. Once, as he was copying a document, he very nearly made a mistake, so that he almost cried out: "Ugh!" and crossed himself. At least once a month he called in on Petrovich to discuss the overcoat, where best to buy the cloth and of what colour and at what price, and he went home, sometimes a bit preoccupied but always contented, thinking of how the time would finally come when the purchase would be made and the overcoat finished. It all went even quicker than he had anticipated. Against every expectation the director allotted Akaky Akakievich not forty or forty-five, but the entire sum of sixty roubles: whether he had a feeling that Akaky Akakievich was in need of a coat, or whether it just happened, he now found himself with an extra twenty roubles. This turn of events accelerated the matter. Another two to three months of light fasting and Akaky Akakievich had indeed accumulated about eighty roubles. His heart, which was usually quite calm, began to pound. The very next available day he went to the shop with Petrovich. They bought some very good cloth – and no wonder, because they had already been thinking about this for half a year, and scarcely a month had gone by without their calling in at the shop to compare prices; and then Petrovich himself said that there was no better cloth to be had. For the lining they chose calico, but of such quality and thickness that, according to Petrovich, it was even better than silk and had an even nicer and glossier look to it. They did not buy marten fur, because it was indeed very expensive, but chose cat fur instead, the best to be found in the shop, cat fur that from a distance could always be taken for marten. Petrovich spent a whole two weeks working on the overcoat, because there was a lot of quilting to do, otherwise it might have been finished sooner. Petrovich took twelve roubles for his work – he could not possibly have charged less: absolutely everything was sewn with silk, with fine double-stitched seams, and Petrovich went over every stitch with his own teeth, impressing different patterns that way.

It was... it is difficult to name the exact day, but it was probably the most glorious day in Akaky Akakievich's life when Petrovich finally brought over the overcoat. He brought it in the morning, before it was time to set off for the office. It could not have come at a better time, because rather heavy frosts had already set in, and they apparently threatened to intensify. Petrovich appeared with the overcoat, as behoves a good tailor. He wore such an solemn expression on his face, the like of which Akaky Akakievich had never seen before. He seemed to feel the full extent of what he had achieved, having now demonstrated the gulf that separates those tailors who insert linings and make repairs from those who sew from scratch. He pulled out the overcoat from a large handkerchief in which he had brought it: the handkerchief was only just back from the laundry, and afterwards he rolled it up and put it in his pocket for further use. Having unwrapped the coat he looked very proud and, holding it in both hands, threw it very deftly onto Akaky Akakievich's shoulders. He then gave it a little pull and smoothed it down from behind with his hand; then he draped it over Akaky Akakievich, leaving it unbuttoned. Akaky Akakievich, being no longer a young man, wanted to try out the sleeves. So Petrovich helped him into his sleeves – it turned out that it also looked good with the sleeves. In a word, the overcoat appeared to be a perfect fit. Petrovich did not miss the opportunity to say at this point that it was only because he lived on a small street, without a shop sign, and also because he had known Akaky Akakievich for a long time, that he had charged so little; on Nevsky Prospect he would have been charged seventy-five roubles for the work alone. Akaky Akakievich did not want to discuss this with Petrovich and was afraid of all those huge sums Petrovich loved to bandy about. He settled with him, thanked him and immediately set off for the office in his new overcoat. Petrovich came out after him and, remaining on the street, looked for a long time at the overcoat from a distance, and then intentionally set off at a right angle so that, by going round a crooked alley, he could run back onto the street and have another look at his overcoat from another angle – that is, facing him. Meanwhile Akaky Akakievich walked along in the most festive of moods. He was aware, every second of every minute, of the new overcoat on his shoulders, and he even smiled at times with inner delight. Indeed there were two benefits: one was that it was warm and the other that it looked good. He did not pay any attention at all to where he was going, and suddenly he found himself at the office. In the porter's lodge he took off his coat, inspected it all over and entrusted it to the porter's special safekeeping. It's not known how everyone in the office suddenly knew that Akaky Akakievich owned a new overcoat and that the "dressing gown" no longer existed. Everyone instantly rushed into the porter's lodge to look at the new coat. They began to congratulate him and cheer him, which at first just made him smile, but then made him even feel embarrassed. When they all moved close up to him and began to say that they should drink to the new overcoat or that, at the very least, he should throw a party for them all, Akaky Akakievich became very flustered; he did not know how to react or respond and how to get out of the situation. After a few minutes or so, turning very red, he was about to assure them rather naively that it wasn't a new overcoat at all, that it was really just his old coat. In the end one of the clerks, some senior clerk's aide in fact, probably to demonstrate that he was not a proud man and was on friendly terms with his inferiors, said: "So be it, I'll have a party instead of Akaky Akakievich and I invite you all to come to me for tea today, for it happens to be my name day." The clerks of course immediately congratulated the senior clerk's aide and eagerly accepted the invitation. Akaky Akakievich was about to excuse himself, but everyone began to say that it was rude, that it was simply shameful and that there was no way he could refuse. Besides, he began to feel pleased when he remembered that he would now have the chance to go out in his new overcoat in the evening too. That entire day was for Akaky Akakievich truly the most glorious day of celebration. He went home in the happiest of moods, took off his coat and carefully hung it on the wall, admiring the cloth and the lining once more, and then, to compare, he purposely took out his old coat that was now completely falling apart. He looked at it and even began to laugh: what a huge difference! And he went on smiling for a long time over dinner every time his old coat's condition came to mind. He had dinner in a cheerful mood, and afterwards did not write anything, not a single document, and just indulged himself a little by lying on his bed while it was still light outside. Then, without further ado, he dressed, put his coat over his shoulders and went out into the street. Where exactly the clerk who had issued the invitation lived we unfortunately can't say:

our memory has begun to fail us badly and everything in St Petersburg, all its streets and houses, have merged and brought about such confusion in our mind that it's very hard to make sense of it all. However that may be, at least there's no doubt that this clerk lived in the better part of town – in fact, at quite a distance from Akaky Akakievich's place. At first Akaky Akakievich had to cross some deserted streets with sparse lighting, but as he came closer to the clerk's apartment the streets became livelier, more populated and more brightly lit. Pedestrians flashed by more often, even prettily dressed ladies began to turn up, beaver collars appeared on men's coats, and cabbies with wooden latticed sleighs stuck with gilt nails cropped up less frequently; on the contrary, you kept on coming across dashing coachmen, wearing crimson velvet hats, in lacquered sleighs with bearskin rugs, or carriages with decked-out driving seats would fly along the street, their wheels screeching across the snow. Akaky Akakievich looked at all this as at something totally unfamiliar. He had for several years now not been out in the streets at night. He stopped inquisitively in front of a lit-up shop window to look at a picture portraying some pretty woman removing her shoe, thus uncovering her whole leg, quite an attractive one at that; behind her, from another doorway, a man with side whiskers and a handsome pointed beard under his lip poked out his head. Akaky Akakievich shook his head and smiled, then continued on his

way. Why did he smile? Was it because he had come across
something completely unfamiliar, but for which, nevertheless,
everyone does harbour some feeling? Or did he think, together
with many other clerks, the following: "Well, really those
French! What can I say, if they're after something, er, then there
it is, er..." or did he perhaps not think that at all – for it's
impossible to get into someone's soul and know all his thoughts.
At last he reached the house where the senior clerk's aide had
lodgings. The senior clerk's aide lived in grand style: the staircase was lit up, and the apartment was on the first floor. As he
came into the hall, Akaky Akakievich saw whole rows of
galoshes on the floor. Among them, in the middle of the room,
stood a samovar, noisily letting out puffs of steam. All along
the walls hung coats and cloaks, some of which even had beaver-
fur collars or velvet lapels. Beyond the wall you could hear noise
and chatter, which suddenly became loud and clear whenever
the door opened and a footman came out with a tray laden
with empty glasses, a cream jug and a basketful of rusks. The
clerks had obviously already come together a while ago and
had drunk their first glass of tea. Akaky Akakievich, after
hanging up his coat himself, entered the room and was confronted all at once by the flash of candles, clerks, pipes and
card tables, and his ears were stunned by the rapid rising sound
of conversation from every corner of the room and the noise
of chairs being moved. He stopped quite awkwardly in the

middle of the room, looking around and trying to think what to do. But he had already been spotted and was greeted with cries, and everyone immediately rushed out to the hall and gave his overcoat another inspection. Akaky Akakievich was partly embarrassed but, being a pure-hearted man, he could not help being glad when he saw how everyone praised his overcoat. Then, of course, they all abandoned both him and his coat and, as these things go, turned to the tables set up for whist. All of this – the noise, the chatter and the crowd of people – was all rather bewildering for Akaky Akakievich. He simply did not know how to behave, where to put his arms and legs or indeed any part of himself. In the end he sat down by the card players, looked at the cards, contemplated the face of this or that player and after a while began to yawn and feel bored, especially as the hour when he usually went to bed had long passed. He wanted to say goodbye to his host, but was not allowed to, being told that a glass of champagne had to be drunk in honour of the new garment. An hour later supper was brought in, consisting of beetroot salad, cold veal, meat pasties, pastries and champagne. They made Akaky Akakievich drink two glasses of champagne, after which he felt that the room had become merrier, but he could not forget, however, that it was already midnight and high time to go home. To stop his host from somehow trying to detain him, he left the room very quietly, looked in the hall for his coat – which, to his chagrin, he saw lying on the floor – gave it a shake, removed any pieces of fluff from it, put it over his shoulders and took the stairway to the street.

Outside it was still bright. Some small shops, those permanent gathering places for servants and all kinds of people, were open, while others which were closed gave off a long strip of light the whole length of the door joint, indicating that there were still people there, probably housemaids and menservants finishing off their gossip and chat, leaving their masters completely in the dark as to their whereabouts. Akaky Akakievich was in a cheerful mood as he walked on and was even, inexplicably, about to run up suddenly to some lady who passed by like a flash and whose body – every particle of it – was filled with extraordinary movement. He did stop himself at once, however, and went on very quietly as before, amazed at himself for that sudden increased pace that had appeared from nowhere. Soon there stretched before him those deserted streets, which even in daytime, let alone in the evening, are not so cheerful. Now they became even more desolate and remote: street lamps appeared less frequently – there was obviously a smaller supply of oil in these parts. From then on there were wooden houses and fences. Not a soul anywhere: only the snow glittered on the streets and small slumbering hovels with closed shutters formed gloomy dark blots. He came near the place where the street was cut across by an endless square that looked like a terrifying desert, the houses on its other side hardly visible.

In the distance, God knows where, a little light flashed in a sentry box that seemed to be standing at the edge of the world. Here Akaky Akakievich's high spirits somehow shrank considerably. He stepped onto the square, not without some instinctive dread, as though his heart had a sense of foreboding. He looked behind and on both sides: it was like a sea all around him. "No, better not to look," he thought, and walked on with his eyes shut, and when he opened them to find out if the end of the square was in sight he suddenly saw that right in front of him, almost under his nose, stood some men with moustaches – but he could not exactly distinguish what they were. His eyes misted over and his heart started pounding in his chest. "Oh look, there's my overcoat!" one of them said in a thunderous voice, grabbing him by the collar. Akaky Akakievich was about to shout for help when another man shoved a fist the size of a clerk's head right up to his mouth, saying: "Don't you dare scream!" Akaky Akakievich only felt them take his coat and kick him with a knee, and he fell backwards in the snow and felt nothing more. A few moments later he came to and got to his feet, but there was no longer anyone around. He felt the cold ground and the lack of his overcoat; he began to shout, but his voice seemed unwilling to reach the far end of the square. Desperate, shouting repeatedly, he began to run across the square straight to the sentry box, next to which stood a sentry leaning on his halberd and apparently looking on with curiosity, keen to know who the Devil it was running and shouting from a distance towards him. Akaky Akakievich ran up to him and began to shout breathlessly that he must have been asleep and not been watching out, that he had not seen a man being robbed. The sentry replied that he'd not seen a thing, that he'd seen how two men had stopped him in the middle of the square, but that he'd taken them to be friends; also that, instead of swearing to no purpose, he'd do better to go to the Police Inspector tomorrow, so that he could find out who'd taken his coat. Akaky Akakievich ran home in complete disarray: his hair, of which he still had a small quantity on his temples and the back of his head, was all dishevelled; his sides and front and trousers were covered in snow. His old landlady, hearing a dreadful knocking at the door, hastily jumped out of bed and ran with only one shoe on to open the door, modestly pressing her nightshirt against her bosom, but having opened the door she jumped back at the sight of the state Akaky Akakievich was in. When he told her what had happened, she clasped her hands together and told him to go straight to the Police Superintendent, that the Inspector would dupe him, would give him assurances and would lead him by the nose. Best of all would be to go straight to the Superintendent; she actually knew him, because Anna, the Finnish woman who used to work for her as a cook now worked as a nanny at the Superintendent's house: she often saw him walking past their house; he went to church every Sunday and prayed, all the while looking cheerfully at everyone – and, all things considered, he must be a good man. Having heard her out, Akaky Akakievich wandered sadly into his room, and how he spent that night I'll leave to the judgement of whoever is able to some degree to imagine himself in someone else's shoes. Early the following morning, he made his way to the Superintendent's, but was told that he was asleep; he came at ten – and they told him again: he's asleep; he came at eleven o'clock – they said that he wasn't at home; and at lunchtime – but the clerks in the lobby would not let him in and absolutely wanted to know on what business he'd come, why he needed to be there and what had happened. So that in the end Akaky Akakievich for once in his life decided to show some character and said point-blank that he had to see the Superintendent in person, that they wouldn't dare not let him in, that he'd come from the Department on official business and that if he put in a complaint about them, then they'd see. Faced with this the clerks did not dare say anything, and one of them went off to call the Superintendent. The Superintendent reacted to the story of the coat robbery in the strangest of ways. Instead of focusing on the main point, he began to question Akaky Akakievich – why had he been going home so late, had he not been in a house of ill repute – so that Akaky Akakievich became totally confused and left the Superintendent not knowing whether the matter of his coat would be pursued in the proper manner. He was not in the office that whole day (the first time in his life). The following day he turned up very pale and in his old "dressing gown" which had become even more pitiful. The tale of the coat robbery did, however, touch many, although even then there were some clerks who did not miss the opportunity of making fun of Akaky Akakievich. They decided there and then to organize a collection for him, but they raised the most trivial amount, because the clerks had spent a lot as it was, subscribing to a portrait of the Director and some book at the suggestion of a departmental head, who was the author's friend – so the sum was a mere trifle. Just one of them, moved by pity, decided to help Akaky Akakievich at least with some good advice, telling him not to go to the Police Inspector, for the reason that even if the Inspector, wishing to earn the approval of the authorities, somehow happened to get hold of the coat, it would nevertheless remain with the police if he did not have legal proof that the coat was his. Best of all would be for him to turn to a certain Important Person, as the Important Person, by writing and getting in touch with the right people, might get the affair to proceed more smoothly. There was nothing for it: Akaky Akakievich decided to go to the Important Person. What the Important Person's job title was or what his role consisted of has remained unknown to this day. What needs to be clear is that a certain Important Person had become an Important Person only recently, and that up till then he had been an Unimportant Person. Besides, his job even now was not regarded as important compared to other ones even more important. But there will always be a circle of people for whom the unimportant in other people's eyes is important for them. Besides, he tried to reinforce his importance by various other means, for example: he established that the lower-ranked civil servants should meet him on the stairs when he came to the office; that no one should dare come straight to him and, to keep everything under the strictest regime, he made the Collegiate Registrar report to the Provincial Secretary, and the Provincial Secretary to the Titular Councillor or whoever else was suitable, so that by this route the matter would finally end up with him. This is how everything in Holy Russia is infected with the art of imitation: everyone mimics and apes his boss. It is even said that a certain Titular Councillor, when made Head of Department in some minor office, immediately partitioned off a particular room calling it an "audience chamber" and put some ushers with red collars and gold braid at the door to grab the door handle and open up to every newcomer, although there was scarcely enough room for an ordinary desk in that "audience chamber". The Important Person's methods and habits were firm and imposing, but not complex. The main basis of his system was strictness. "Strictness, strictness and – strictness," he would usually say, and at the last word he would look very pointedly into the face of the person he was addressing. Although, by the way, there was no reason at all for this, because the dozen or so clerks who made up the whole administrative machine of the office were in a state of suitable awe anyway. Whenever they spotted the boss from a distance, they stopped their work and stood to attention while he walked across the room. His usual conversation with his underlings was imbued with strictness and consisted mostly of three phrases: "How dare you? Do you know who you're speaking to? Do you understand who it is standing before you?" He was, however, a kind man at heart, pleasant with his friends and helpful, but the rank of general had thrown him totally off balance. Upon obtaining the rank of general, he somehow became confused, lost his way and had no idea how to behave. If he happened to be with his equals, he still behaved decently, a very respectable man and in many ways quite an intelligent man, but as soon as he happened to find himself in the company of people of only one rank below him, he was no good at all: he remained silent and his situation excited pity, all the more so because even he himself felt that he could be spending his time in an incomparably better way. Sometimes you could see in his eyes a strong desire to join some interesting conversation or group of people, but he would be held back by the thought:

would it be a step too far on his part, would it not be over-familiar and would he discredit his own importance that way? Following such reasoning he constantly remained in that silent state, only rarely pronouncing a one-syllable sound, and so he acquired the reputation of being the dullest of men. It was to such an Important Person that our Akaky Akakievich appeared, and he appeared at the most inauspicious time, quite inopportunely for himself, though in fact very opportunely for the Important Person. The Important Person was in his office and was chatting very, very happily with an old acquaintance, a childhood friend who had recently arrived and whom he had not seen for several years. At that moment it was announced that a certain Bashmachkin had come. He asked abruptly: "Who's that?"

"Some clerk," was the reply.

"Oh! He can wait, now's not the time," the Important Person said. It must be said here that the Important Person was telling a complete fib: he did have time – he and his friend had already talked over everything and interspersed the conversation with lengthy silences, just lightly tapping each other's thigh from time to time saying: "So, Ivan Abramovich!" – "Just so, Stepan Varlamovich!" He nevertheless asked the clerk to wait in order to show his friend, a man who had long stopped working and was living in the country, how long clerks would wait for him in the hall. Finally, after quite enough talking and rather more silent moments, and after smoking a cigar in very comfortable armchairs with adjustable backs, he finally, as though he had suddenly remembered, told his secretary who was standing by the door with documents for a report: "Ah yes, there's a clerk out there, I believe; tell him to come in." Seeing Akaky Akakievich's meek countenance and old uniform, he suddenly turned to him and said: "What do you want?" with an abrupt and firm voice, which he had purposely taught himself, alone in his room in front of the mirror, a week before receiving his present post and the rank of general. Akaky Akakievich, who had already been suffering in anticipation from a shyness that accorded properly with the occasion, became a bit confused and, as best he could, in so far as his fluency of tongue would let him, explained – adding the interjection "er" even more frequently than usual – that the overcoat was completely new and had been stolen in brutal fashion, and that he was turning to him so that with his intercession he could, er, somehow or other communicate by letter with the Chief of Police, or someone else, to find the overcoat. For some inexplicable reason, the General regarded such manner of address as too familiar.

"What are you saying, my dear sir?" he said, still abruptly. "Don't you know the form? Whose office you've entered? Don't you know how things are done? You should first have put in a request at the chancellery; it would have gone on to the Senior Clerk, to the Head of Department, then passed on to the Secretary and only then would the Secretary have brought it to me…"

"But Your Excellency," Akaky Akakievich said, trying to muster whatever presence of mind he had left in him and feeling at the same time that he was sweating profusely, "I took it upon myself to trouble Your Excellency, because the secretaries, er… unreliable people…"

"What, what, what?" said the Important Person. "Where did you get the nerve? Where did you get such ideas? What is this unruliness which has spread among young people against their bosses and superiors!"

The Important Person had seemingly not noticed that Akaky Akakievich was already well over fifty. So that if he could be called a young man, then it could only be done in comparison – that is, compared to someone who is already seventy.

"Do you know whom you are speaking to? Do you understand who it is standing before you? Do you understand, do you understand? I'm asking you."

And he stamped his foot, raising his voice to such heights that even someone other than Akaky Akakievich would have been terrified. Akaky Akakievich went numb; he tottered, his whole body started shaking, and he could not stay on his feet. Had the porters not run forward to get hold of him he would have tumbled to the ground; they carried him away almost lifeless. And the Important Person, pleased that the effect had even exceeded his expectations, and totally delighted at the thought that his words could even deprive a man of his senses, gave his friend a sideways glance to see how he took this, and he saw, not without some satisfaction, that his friend was in some confusion and had even begun to feel afraid himself.

How he came down the stairs, how he came out into the street, none of this did Akaky Akakievich remember. He could not feel his arms or legs. He had never in his life been given such a reprimand by a general, and a stranger to him at that. He walked through the storm that whistled down the streets, his mouth gaping, straying off the pavement. The wind, as it does in St Petersburg, blew at him from all four corners, from all side streets. His throat was instantly beset by a severe infection, and he made it home without any strength left to utter a single word. He swelled up all over and took to his bed. That is how powerful a proper reprimand can be! The very next day he was in the throes of a very high fever. Thanks to the magnanimous assistance of the Petersburg climate, the illness progressed more swiftly than might have been expected, and when the doctor appeared and had felt his pulse, he could find nothing more to do than to prescribe a poultice, only to ensure that the patient should not be left without the benefit of medical aid. He nevertheless announced that within thirty-six hours it would definitely be the end of him. After that he turned to the landlady and said: "You, dearie, don't waste time, order him a pine coffin now, because an oak one will be too expensive for him." Whether Akaky Akakievich heard those fatal words, and if he did hear them, whether they had a shattering effect on him, whether he regretted his wretched life – none of this is known, because he was in a continuous state of delirium and fever. He constantly had visions, one stranger than the next: in one he saw Petrovich and ordered him to make an overcoat with some kinds of traps for robbers whom he kept on seeing under the bed, and he would summon the landlady every minute to pull out a robber from under his blanket; in another he asked why his old "dressing gown" was hanging in front of him, as he had a new overcoat; in another he imagined himself standing before the General, listening to his rightful reprimand and saying: "I'm guilty, Your Excellency!" In the end he even used foul language, uttering the most horrid words so that the landlady actually crossed herself, having never heard anything like it from him before, especially as those words directly followed the words "Your Excellency". He went on speaking complete nonsense, impossible to understand; you could only see that the confused words and thoughts revolved round the one and only overcoat. At last poor Akaky Akakievich gave up the ghost. Neither his room nor his belongings were given an official seal,* because, firstly, he had no heirs and secondly, there was very little left, namely: a bundle of goose feathers, two dozen sheets of official white paper, three pairs of socks, two or three buttons that had been torn off his trousers and the "dressing gown" already known to the reader. Who it all eventually ended up with God only knows: even the teller of this tale, I must confess, showed no interest in this. They took Akaky Akakievich away and buried him. And St Petersburg was left without Akaky Akakievich, as though he had never been there. So vanished without trace a creature with no one to defend him, dear to no one, of no interest to anyone, who did not even attract the attention of a naturalist who would never miss an opportunity to pin down a common fly and inspect it through a microscope; a creature who had humbly endured office taunts and who went to his grave without undue fuss, but for whom nevertheless, although at the very end of his life, a bright visitor had made a fleeting appearance in the guise of an overcoat, livening up for an instant a miserable life, and upon whom misfortune then fell as unendurably as it falls upon kings and world sovereigns... A few days after his death a porter from his department was sent to the apartment with the order that he should immediately come to the office: the Head of Department himself demanded this, but the porter had to return without anything, reporting that Akaky Akakievich could no longer come, and to the query as to why he expressed himself with these words: "Well, he just can't as he's dead; he was buried three days ago." That was the way they found out about Akaky Akakievich's death in the department, and the following day a new clerk sat in his place, much taller and no longer forming his letters in a straight hand, but in a much more slanting one.

But who could have imagined that this was not the last to be said about Akaky Akakievich, that he was destined to live on noisily for a few days after his death, as though in reward for a life overlooked by all? Yet that is what happened, and our sad tale unexpectedly takes on a fantasy ending. Rumours suddenly spread across St Petersburg that, near Kalinkin Bridge and far beyond, a corpse in the guise of a clerk had begun to appear by night, looking for a certain stolen coat and, under pretext of that stolen coat, ripping every coat off every shoulder, irrespective of rank or title: coats of cat fur, beaver, wadded coats, raccoon, fox, bear – in a word, of every kind of fur and skin that people have thought up to cover themselves with. One of the departmental clerks saw the corpse with his own eyes and immediately recognized Akaky Akakievich, but this filled him with such terror that he ran off as fast as his legs could carry him and was therefore unable to have a good look and only saw that it shook its finger at him from a distance. Constant complaints came from all quarters that backs and shoulders, not only those of titular, but even of some privy councillors, had been subjected to real chills because of this nocturnal removal of overcoats. The police were instructed to catch the corpse at any price, dead or alive, and to punish it, as an example to others, in the most severe manner, and they did almost succeed. In fact a policeman of a certain district was about to grab the corpse firmly by the collar in the Kiriushnik Alley, at the very spot of the crime, as it attempted to pull off the woollen coat of some retired musician who in his day had whistled on a flute. Having grabbed it by the collar, he called out loudly for two of his colleagues and ordered them to hold on to it, whilst he himself reached into his boot for only a moment to pull out his birch-bark snuffbox and briefly revive his nose that had been slightly frostbitten six times in his lifetime; but the tobacco was obviously of a kind that even a corpse could not bear. The policeman, having pressed his finger against his right nostril, had barely managed to sniff half a handful into his left one, when the corpse sneezed so hard that it completely bespattered the eyes of all three men. During the time it took to lift their fists to wipe them, the corpse vanished without a trace, so that they did not even know whether they had actually held it at all. From then on the policemen had such a fear of dead men that they even avoided catching live ones and only called out from a distance: "Hey, you, on your way!" – and the dead clerk began to appear even beyond the Kalinkin Bridge, inspiring terror in all fearful folk. We have, however, completely left a certain Important Person behind, who indeed was very nearly the reason for the fantastical course of this nevertheless absolutely true story. First of all, for the sake of truth, I'm required to say that a certain Important Person, soon after the exit of the poor, utterly rebuked Akaky Akakievich, felt some sort of regret. He was no stranger to compassion; his heart was open to many good impulses, despite the fact that his rank often stopped them from manifesting themselves. As soon as his friend had left his office he even fell to thinking about poor Akaky Akakievich. And from then on almost every day a pale Akaky Akakievich, incapable of enduring an official reprimand, appeared before him. This thought troubled him so much that a week later he even decided to send a clerk to him to find out what he wanted and how he was and whether there was indeed a way to help him, and when they reported back to him that Akaky Akakievich had suddenly died of a fever, he felt overwhelmed and guilt-ridden and was out of sorts all that day. Wishing somehow to find distraction and forget the unpleasant impression, he made his way to an evening party given by one of his friends, where he found a decent gathering and, even better, everyone there was more or less of the same rank, so that he could be totally himself. This had an amazing effect on his spirits. He let himself go: he was pleasant in conversation, amiable – in short, he spent a very pleasant evening. At supper he drank two glasses of champagne – which, as you know, has a positive convivial effect. The champagne instilled him with a mood for various extravagant undertakings and, specifically, he decided not to go home yet, but to visit a certain friend, Karolina Ivanovna, a lady, it seems, of German origin, with whom he felt on very friendly terms. It has to be said that the Important Person was no longer a young man and was a good husband and a respectable paterfamilias. Two sons, one of whom already worked in the office, and a sweet-faced sixteen-year-old daughter with a slightly upturned but cute little nose came each morning to kiss his hand, saying: "*Bonjour, Papa.*" His wife, a still youthful and even good-looking woman, first gave him her hand to be kissed and then, turning her hand round, kissed his hand. But the Important Person, perfectly contented, by the way, with his family's affectionate ways, found it becoming to have friendly relations with a lady friend on the other side of town. This friend was neither better nor younger than his wife, but such are the ways of the world, and it's not for us to judge. So the Important Person came down the stairs, sat down in his sleigh and told the driver: "To Karolina Ivanovna's," and, wrapping himself luxuriously in his warm overcoat, he remained in that pleasant state, which has no rival for a Russian – that is, when you think of nothing and meanwhile thoughts come leaping into your head of their own accord, each one more appealing than the other, without having to chase them up or look for them. Filled with contentment, he gently brought to mind all the happy instances of that evening, all the words that had made the small group roar with laughter. He even repeated many of them in a whisper and found them just as funny as before, and so it's no wonder that he would chuckle heartily himself. He was, however, now and then disturbed by a blustery wind which, suddenly appearing from God knows where and for no apparent reason, cut him right across the face, chucking snow up at him, turning up his coat collar like a sail or suddenly throwing it back on his head with extraordinary power, giving him endless trouble when freeing himself of it. All of a sudden the Important Person felt himself being grabbed very forcefully by the collar. As he turned round, he saw a small person in an old worn uniform and he recognized, not without terror, Akaky Akakievich. The clerk's face was as pale as snow and looked like a real corpse. But the Important Person's terror knew no bounds when he saw the corpse's mouth become twisted and, exuding a terrible smell of the grave, pronounce these words: "Ah! There you are at last! I've got you at last, er, by the collar! It's your coat I need! You didn't bother about mine and even reprimanded me – hand yours over right now!" The poor Important Person nearly died. However much he displayed a strong character in the office, mostly with his subordinates, and although everyone would say, when you merely looked at his manly appearance and figure: "Oh what a character!" – here, as happens with many who look heroic, he was overcome by such terror, not without reason, he even began to fear having a seizure of some sort.

He actually threw his coat off his shoulders as quickly as possible and shouted to the driver in a voice not his own: "Take me home at top speed!" The driver, hearing a tone of voice mostly used at critical moments and usually accompanied by something much more physical, buried his head in his shoulders to be on the safe side, brandished his whip and shot off like an arrow. Within just over six minutes the Important Person was already by his front porch. Pale, scared and coatless, he had come to his own house, instead of calling in at Karolina Ivanovna's. He somehow dragged himself to his bedroom and spent the whole night in great turmoil, so much so that the next morning over tea his daughter said to him outright: "You're very pale today, Papa." But Papa kept silent and told no one about what had happened, where he had been and where he had intended to go. That experience made a strong impression on him. He would in fact far less often say to his subordinates: "How dare you? Do you understand who it is standing before you?" – and if he did say so, it was not before hearing what the issue was. But still more amazing is that from then on the dead clerk stopped appearing: the General's overcoat evidently fitted him really well. At least there were no more incidents anywhere of someone's overcoat being ripped off. However, many restless and solicitous people simply refused to be reassured and said that the dead clerk still appeared in distant corners of the city. And indeed, a policeman of Kolomna saw with his own eyes a ghost appear from behind a house, but being somewhat feeble by nature – so much so that an ordinary fully grown young pig had once, making a dash out of a private house, knocked him over, to the great merriment of some coachmen standing around, for which insult he had levied from each one of them half a copeck for snuff – and so, being feeble, he did not dare to stop it, but just kept following it in the dark until at last the ghost suddenly looked back, stopped and asked: "What do you want?" – and raised such a fist as you'll never even find among the living. "Nothing," the policeman said, and immediately turned back. The ghost, however, was a lot taller by now and had a huge moustache – and, apparently heading towards Obukhov Bridge, vanished completely into the darkness of the night.

Diary of a Madman

SOMETHING EXTRAORDINARY happened today. I got up rather late in the morning, and when Mavra brought me my polished boots, I asked her what the time was. When I heard that it was well past ten o'clock, I hurried to get dressed. I confess I would rather not have gone to the office at all, as I knew beforehand what a sour face our Head of Department would pull. He's long been saying to me: "Why is your head always in such a muddle, old chap? At times you rush about like one possessed and sometimes you make such a mess of the matter in hand that the Devil himself couldn't make head or tail of it; you use a lower-case letter in a title and you don't write down the date or number." Cursed heron! He's probably envious of the fact that I sit in the Director's office and sharpen His Excellency's quills.* In a word, I wouldn't have gone to the office had I not hoped to meet the bursar and perhaps wangle some advance on my salary out of that Jew. Now there's another personage! Good God, Judgement Day will be upon us before he'll ever hand over any monthly advance. You may ask till you're blue in the face, even if you're in dire straits – that grey-haired devil won't give you a thing. Yet, at

143

home his own cook slaps him across the cheeks. That's common knowledge. I don't understand the advantages of working in our department. There are no fringe benefits at all. It's a different matter altogether in the provincial administration, in the Civil and Treasury Offices: there you'll spot someone squeezed into a corner scribbling away. He wears a vile tailcoat, his mug is such that it makes you want to spit, but look at the kind of dacha he rents! Don't bring him a gilt china teacup: "That," he says, "is the kind of gift for a doctor." Give him rather a pair of horses or a droshky or a beaver fur worth about three hundred roubles. He has such a muted expression and speaks so delicately: "Please lend me your little knife to sharpen my little quill," and then he proceeds to strip the petitioner of all but his shirt. It's true, our own service is noble, there's cleanliness everywhere such as would not be seen for years in the provincial administration: the desks are all made of mahogany and all the superiors use the polite form of address. Yes, I do admit that were it not for the nobility* of our service, I would have left the office long ago.

I put on my old overcoat and took an umbrella, because it was pouring with rain. There was no one on the streets; I only caught sight of peasant women sheltering under their coat skirts, Russian merchants under umbrellas and messenger boys. Of the gentry there was only one fellow clerk trudging along. I spotted him at the crossroads. As soon as I saw him I said to myself: "Aha! My friend, you're not on your way to the office: you're just hurrying after the girl who's running ahead of you, and you're staring at her little feet." What a beast our brother clerk is! Honestly, he won't give way to any officer: some woman in a hat comes by and he'll definitely hook on to her. As I was thinking this, I caught sight of a carriage driving up to the shop I was walking past. I instantly recognized it. It was our director's carriage. "But he has no business in the shop," I thought. "It's probably his daughter." I pressed myself against the wall. A footman opened the carriage doors, and out she fluttered like a little bird. How she glanced left and right, how she flashed with her eyebrows and eyes... Lord, my God! I'm done for, I'm utterly done for. Why did she have to go out in such rainy weather! Now tell me that women don't have a huge passion for all this finery. She didn't recognize me, and I deliberately tried to wrap up as tightly as possible, because I wore a very grubby overcoat, and an old-fashioned one at that. They now wear cloaks with long collars and mine is short and overlapping – and the fabric isn't waterproof at all. Her little dog didn't make it through the shop entrance and stayed outside. I know that little dog. She's called Madgie. I'd hardly been there a minute when I suddenly heard a high-pitched little voice: "Hello, Madgie!" Fancy that! Who was saying that? I looked round and saw two ladies walking by under an umbrella: an old one and a young one, but they'd already gone past when again a voice rang out near me: "Shame on you, Madgie!" What the Devil! I saw Madgie and a small dog that followed the ladies sniffing round each other. "Aha!" I said to myself. "Enough of this, could I be drunk? But that rarely happens to me."

"No, Fidèle, you shouldn't think that." I actually saw Madgie saying. "I've been, woof-woof, I've been, woof-woof-woof, very ill." Really, you little dog! I confess that I was extremely surprised to hear her speak like a human being. But later, when I figured all this out carefully, I stopped being surprised. Indeed, many similar examples have occurred in the world. They say that in England there was a fish that swam to the surface and said two words in some strange language, and that scholars have been trying for three years to decipher them and haven't discovered anything to this day. I've also read in the papers about two cows that came up to a stall and asked for a pound of tea. But I confess that I was much more surprised when Madgie said: "I wrote to you, Fidèle; I suppose that Polkan didn't deliver my letter!" May I forfeit my pay, but I've never in my life heard of a dog being able to write. Only a gentleman can write properly. Well, of course some merchant clerks and even some serfs occasionally scribble, but their writing is mostly mechanical: no commas, no full stops, no style.

I was amazed. I must confess that at times of late I've begun to hear and see things such as no one has seen or heard of before.

I think I might follow that little dog, I said to myself, to find out what she's like and what she might be thinking. I unfolded my umbrella and set off after the two ladies. They crossed over to Gorokhovaya Street, turned into Meshchanskaya Street, from there on to Stolyarnaya Street, finally to Kokushkin Bridge, and then stopped in front of a large house. "I know that house," I said to myself. "It's Zverkov's house."* What a set-up! The people that live there: the number of cooks and guests! As for our fellow clerks, they sit one on top of the other like dogs. A friend of mine is there: a good trumpet player. The ladies went up to the fifth floor. "Good," I thought. "I won't go there now, but will take note of the place and won't fail to make use of it at the first opportunity."

4th October

Today is Wednesday, which is why I went to our head of department's office. I deliberately came in earlier and, having sat down, re-sharpened all the quills. Our director must be a very clever man. His whole study consists of shelves lined with books. I read some of the titles: it's all learning, learning quite beyond our fellow clerk: it's all either in French or German. And to look at his face: oh, such importance shines through his eyes! I've never heard him use a superfluous word. Only when you pass him some documents he'll ask: "What's it like outside?"

"It's wet, Your Excellency!"

No, he can't be compared to the likes of us! A true states-
man. I've noticed, however, that he particularly likes me. If
only his daughter... Oh, how shocking! Never mind, never
mind, silence! I read the *Little Bee*.* What fools those French!*
So what do they want? I'd take hold of each one of them, by
Jove, and flog them with birch rods! I also read a very pleasing
portrayal of a ball, described by a landowner from Kursk;*
landowners from Kursk write well. After that I noticed that the
clock had already struck half-past twelve and our director had
not yet left his bedroom. But around half-past one something
happened which no pen can describe. The door opened and
I thought it was the director and jumped up from my chair
with the documents; but it was her, her! Holy Fathers, how she
was dressed! She wore a white dress, like a swan; oh, such a
magnificent one! And what a look she gave: my God, sunshine,
pure sunshine! She nodded and said:" Has *Papa* not been?" Oh,
oh, what a voice! A little canary, truly, a little canary!! "Your
Excellency," I wanted to say, "don't have me executed, or if
you want, execute me with your own superior little hand."
But, damn it, somehow my tongue wouldn't move, and all I
said was: "No, ma'am." She stared at me for a while, then at
the books, and dropped her handkerchief. I rushed forward,
slipped on the damned parquet floor and very nearly got my
nose unstuck, but I did hold on and got the handkerchief. Saints
above, what a handkerchief! Of the finest linen – ambergris,

pure ambergris! It simply exuded high society. She thanked me and gave a half-smile in a way that made her sugar-sweet lips barely move, and left after that. I sat for another hour, when all of a sudden a footman came in and said: "Go home, Aksenty Ivanovich, the master has already left." I can't stand the likes of footmen: they're always lounging around in the entrance hall and they could at least take the trouble to acknowledge you. And that's not all: once one of those louts thought of treating me to snuff without getting off his chair. Don't you know, you stupid lackey, that I'm a civil servant, a man of noble parentage? However, I took my hat and put on my coat myself, because those gentlemen won't help you, and went out. At home I spent most of the time lying on my bed. Then I copied out some very good verses:

> I didn't see my darling for an hour,
> And that to me felt truly like a year;
> I hated what my life had now become,
> To be alive was more than wearisome.

It had to be one of Pushkin's* works. In the evening, wrapped tightly in my coat, I walked to Her Excellency's entrance porch and waited a long time to see if she might come out to her carriage, to be able to look at her just once more – but no, she didn't come out.

6th November

The Head of Department was furious. When I arrived in the office, he summoned me and began to talk to me in this way: "Well, tell me, please, what you are up to?"

"What do you mean? I'm not up to anything." I replied.

"Well, just think about it! You're over forty after all – it's time you got some sense. Who do you think you are? You think I'm not aware of all your tricks? You're running after the director's daughter, it's obvious! Just look at yourself, just think, what are you? You're a nobody, nothing more. You haven't a copeck to your name. Just have a look at your face in the mirror: how could you even think of such a thing!" What the Devil, his face is like a chemist's phial, and on his head he has a wisp of hair tied in a topknot, and he holds his head up and oils it with some kind of pomade and thinks he can do anything. I understand, I do understand why he's angry with me: he's envious. Perhaps he's seen me receive preferential treatment. I spit on him! Such great self-importance for a mere court councillor! He's hung a gold chain from his watch, he orders boots priced at thirty roubles – the Devil take him! Am I from some plebeian family, son of a tailor or a non-commissioned officer? I'm a nobleman. I too can get promoted after all. I'm only forty-two, the time when real service begins. Just you wait, my friend! Even we will be a colonel, and perhaps something more, God willing. We too will get a reputation – and a better one than yours. What were you thinking? That besides you there are no respectable men around? Give me a Ruch's tailcoat,* tailored in the latest fashion, and I'll put on a similar necktie to yours and you wouldn't be a patch on me. I'm just not well off, that's the problem.

8th November

I went to the theatre. They played *Filatka*,* the Russian fool. I laughed a lot. There was some other vaudeville with funny verses about lawyers, and particularly about a certain collegiate registrar, all this written quite freely, so much so that I was amazed they passed the censors; and they spoke openly about merchants, how they deceive people and how their children lead a dissolute life and wriggle their way into the nobility. There was also a very funny couplet about journalists, saying they like to have a go at everything, and the author was asking the public for protection. Our present-day authors produce some very funny plays. I love going to the theatre. As soon as half a copeck turns up in my pocket, nothing will stop me from going. But among our fellow clerks there are such swine: they'll definitely not go to the theatre, the peasants, unless you were to give them a free ticket. One actress sang beautifully. I was reminded of the other... oh, how shocking!... Never mind, never mind... silence.

9th November

I went to the office at eight o'clock. The Head of Department looked as though he hadn't noticed my arrival. I too, for my part, acted as though nothing had happened between us. I checked and sorted out some documents. I left at four. I walked past the Director's apartment, but there was no one to be seen. After dinner I spent most of the time lying on my bed.

11th November

Today I sat in our director's study and sharpened twenty-three quills for him and for her – oh! oh!… – for Her Excellency four quills. He particularly likes having a lot of quills handy. Oh! He must have a fine brain! He keeps silent, but I believe that he considers everything in his head. I'd like to find out what he thinks about most of all, what he's scheming in that head of his. I'd like to examine the lives of these gentlemen closer up, all those double entendres and goings-on at court, how and what they do within their circle – that's what I'd like to know! I've several times thought of starting up a conversation with His Excellency – only, damn it, my tongue wouldn't obey: all I'd say was whether it was cold or warm outside, and definitely nothing else. I'd like to peep into the drawing room, where only sometimes you see an open door, to another room beyond the drawing room. Oh what rich furniture! What mirrors and porcelain! I'd like to peep over there in that part, where Her

Excellency is – that's where I'd want to look! Into the boudoir, how it's full of all those jars, phials and such flowers that you'd be scared of breathing on them, how her discarded dress lies there, more like air than a dress. I'd like to peep into her bedroom... There, I think, there are wonders; there, I think, it's paradise, such as doesn't exist even in heaven. Could I but see the small stool she places her little foot on as she gets up from bed, how she slips a snow-white stocking on that little foot... Oh! Oh! Oh! Never mind, never mind... silence.

Today, however, something suddenly dawned on me: I recalled the conversation between the two little dogs that I'd heard on Nevsky Prospect. "Good," I thought to myself, "I'll now find out everything. I must get hold of the correspondence going on between those wretched little dogs. I'll surely find out something that way." I must confess I've even once called Madgie over and said: "Listen, Madgie, we're on our own now – if you want I'll even lock the door so that no one can see us – tell me everything you know about your mistress, how and what she is. I swear to you that I won't tell anyone." But the cunning little dog put her tail between her legs, shrank into herself and quietly went out the door, as though she'd heard nothing. I've long suspected dogs of being cleverer than people; I've even been convinced that they could speak, but that they were being stubborn. They're exceptional politicians: they notice everything, every step a person takes. No, whatever it takes, I'll go to Zverkov's house tomorrow and I'll question Fidèle – and if I can, I'll grab hold of all the letters Madgie has written to her.

12th November

At two o'clock in the afternoon I set off deliberately to see Fidèle and question her. I can't stand cabbage, with its smell pouring out of every small shop in Meshchanskaya Street. Besides, there's such a hellish stink coming from beneath the gates of every house that I ran at top speed, holding my nose. And petty craftsmen release such a quantity of soot and smoke from their workshops that it's definitely impossible for a gentleman to stroll around here. When I made it to the sixth floor and rang the doorbell, a girl came out, quite a pretty one with tiny freckles. I recognized her. She was the one who'd walked by with the old lady. She blushed slightly and I instantly realized: "You, sweetheart, want a suitor."

"What can I do for you?" she said.

"I need to speak with your little dog."

The girl was stupid! I knew at once that she was stupid. Meanwhile, the little dog came running in, barking. I wanted to grab hold of her, but she, odious thing, almost sank her teeth into my nose. I spotted her basket, however, in a corner. Now that's what I was after! I walked over, poked around in the straw in the wooden box and, to my extraordinary delight, pulled out a small bundle of notelets. That foul little dog, when she saw this, at first bit me on the calf, and then, when she sniffed out that I'd taken the papers, began to whine and grovel, but I said: "No, sweetheart, goodbye!" and ran off. I think the girl took me for a madman, because she was extremely frightened. Having arrived home I wanted to get on right away with the task in hand and sort out the letters, because I don't see very well by candlelight. But Mavra took it into her head to wash the floor. These stupid Finnish women are always given to cleaning at the wrong time. So I went off for a stroll to consider what had just happened. I'll now at last find out all their affairs and thoughts, what makes them tick, and get to the bottom of it all. These letters will reveal all. Dogs are clever folk: they know all the political connections, and so it'll surely all be there: his portrayal and all matters to do with that man. There'll also be something about her, the one who... never mind, silence! I came home by evening. I spent most of the time lying on my bed.

13th November

Well, let's have a look: the letter is quite legible. Still, there's something canine about the handwriting. Let's read:

Dear Fidèle, I still can't get used to your bourgeois name. As if they really couldn't have given you a better one? Fidèle, Rose – how vulgar! Still let's leave all of that aside. I'm very glad that we've decided to write to each other.

The letter is written very correctly. The punctuation and every letter in place. Even our Head of Department doesn't write like that, although he tells us that he studied at a university somewhere. Let's go on:

I feel that sharing thoughts, feelings and impressions with someone else is one of the main pleasures in this world.

Hm! That thought is drawn from a work translated from the German. The title escapes me.

I speak from experience, although I've not been beyond the gates of our house. Is my life not one of pleasure? My mistress, whom Papa calls Sophie, loves me to distraction.

Oh, oh!... Never mind, never mind. Silence!

Papa often fondles me too. I drink tea and coffee with cream. Oh, ma chère, I have to tell you that I see no enjoyment at all in those large gnawed bones which our Polkan chews on in the kitchen.

The only bones that are good are those from wild game, and then only before anyone has sucked out the marrow. It's very good to blend some sauces together, but only without adding capers or greens. But I don't know of anything worse than the

habit of giving dogs little balls made of bread. Some gentle-
man sitting at the table, who has held all kinds of rubbish in
his hands, starts to knead some bread with those hands, calls
you over and shoves the ball in between your teeth. To refuse
seems impolite, so you eat it, with disgust, but you eat it…

The Devil knows what this is! Such nonsense! As though there
wasn't a better subject to write about. Let's look at another
page. There might be something more sensible there.

I'm very ready to inform you of everything that happens in
our house. I've already told you something about the main
gentleman whom Sophie calls Papa. *He's a very strange man.*

Ah! Now at last! I knew it: they have a political outlook on
every subject. Let's see what there is about *Papa*:

…a very strange man. He's mainly silent. He speaks very
rarely; but a week ago he kept on talking to himself: "Will
I or won't I get it?" He takes a piece of paper in one hand
and he clenches the other empty one and says: "Will I or
won't I get it?" He even once turned to me with the ques-
tion: "What do you think, Madgie? Will I or won't I get it?"
I really couldn't understand a thing and sniffed his boot and
went out. Then, ma chère, Papa *came in very elated. Men in*

uniform came to see him all morning and congratulated him about something. He was so cheerful at dinner as I'd never seen him before, told jokes and after dinner he lifted me to his neck and said: "Ah, look Madgie, at this." I saw some kind of ribbon. I sniffed it, but could find no smell at all; in the end I furtively licked it: a bit salty.

Hm! I think that little dog is really too... she could be in for a flogging! Ah! So he's ambitious! This needs to be recorded.

Goodbye, ma chère, I'm off, etc., etc.... I'll finish the letter tomorrow. Well, hello, I'm back with you. Today my mistress Sophie...

Ah! Let's see about Sophie. Oh, how shocking!... Never mind, never mind, we'll go on.

...my mistress Sophie was in quite a state. She was getting ready for a ball and I was looking forward to being able to write to you in her absence. My Sophie is always extremely happy to go to a ball, although when dressing she's always rather irritable. I can't understand at all, ma chère, the pleasure of going to a ball. Sophie usually gets home from the ball at six o'clock in the morning, and I can almost always guess from her pale gaunt look that she's not been given anything

to eat, poor thing. I confess I couldn't ever live that way. If they didn't give me sauce with some hazel grouse or roast chicken wings then... I don't know what would become of me. Sauce with porridge is tasty too. Whilst carrots, turnips or artichokes will never taste nice...

An extremely uneven style. It's immediately obvious that it's not written by a human being. It begins appropriately and ends in doggy style. Let's have a look at another letter. It's rather a long one. Hm! And there's no date.

Oh, my dear! How palpable is the approach of spring. My heart throbs as though it's waiting for something. There's a constant hum in my ears, so that I often stand for a few minutes lifting up one paw and listening at the door. I'll reveal to you that I have many suitors. Sitting by the window, I often have a good look at them. Oh, if you only knew what monstrosities there are among them. One extremely clumsy one, a mongrel, terribly stupid, with stupidity written all over his face, walks very importantly along the street and imagines himself to be a highly distinguished individual; he thinks that everyone is looking at him. Not one bit. I even ignored him as though I hadn't seen him. And what a terrifying mastiff stops at my window! If he stood on his hind legs – which the brute is probably incapable of doing – then he'd be a whole head taller than my Sophie's papa, who himself is quite tall and chunky. That blockhead must be a terribly insolent creature. I growled at him, but it had no effect. He could at least have winced! He stuck out his tongue, hung his huge ears and looked through the window – such a peasant! But perhaps you think, ma chère, that my heart remains indifferent to every request – oh, no… If you could only see one admirer, called Trésor, who climbed over the neighbour's fence! Oh, ma chère, what a cute little snout he has!

Ugh, to hell with it.!… What nonsense!… How can you fill letters with such rubbish? Give me a human being! I want to see a human being; I demand sustenance – of the kind that would nourish and charm my soul; instead of which such nonsense… Let's turn the page to see whether there's any improvement:

…Sophie sat at the table with some sewing. I was looking out of the window, because I enjoy watching passers-by, when suddenly the footman came in and said: "Teplov!"

"Show him in," called out Sophie, and she rushed to hug me… "Oh, Madgie, Madgie! If you but knew who that is: a dark-haired Kammerjunker,* and such eyes! Dark and brightly lit like fire." And Sophie ran into her room. A moment later a young Kammerjunker came in with black side whiskers, and he walked to the mirror, smoothed his

*hair and glanced round the room. I growled a little and sat in
my place. Sophie soon came out and curtsied joyfully to his
clicking heels, and meanwhile I went on looking out through
the window as though unaware of anything; I did however
cock my head a little to one side trying to catch what they
were talking about. Oh,* ma chère, *what trivialities they spoke
about! They spoke about how one lady at the dance had
performed one figure rather than another; also how a certain
Bobov with his jabot looked very much like a stork and had
almost fallen over; that a certain Lidina fancied herself to
have blue eyes whilst they were actually green, and more of
the same. "What would result," I thought to myself, "if you
compared the* Kammerjunker *with Trésor! Heavens! What
a difference! Firstly the* Kammerjunker *has a perfectly broad
smooth face surrounded by side whiskers, as if he'd band-
aged it with a black scarf, whilst Trésor has a slim little snout
and a white spot on his forehead. It's impossible to compare
Trésor's waist with that of the* Kammerjunker's. *As for their
eyes, their ways and manners, they're not at all the same. Oh
what a difference! I don't know,* ma chère, *what she sees in
her Teplov. Why is she so taken with him?*

I myself think that something is not as it should be here. It's
not possible that a *Kammerjunker* could fascinate her so.
Let's continue:

It seems to me that if she likes this Kammerjunker *then she'll soon like that clerk who sits in* Papa's *office. Oh,* ma chère, *if you only knew how ugly that one is. A real tortoise in his shell…*

What clerk could that be?

He has a very strange surname. He always sits and sharpens quills. His hair is very much like hay. Papa *is always sending him off on errands, instead of the servants…*

I think that that disgusting little dog is alluding to me. Since when is my hair like hay?

Sophie can't stop laughing when she looks at him.

You're lying, you accursed little dog! What a vicious tongue! As though I didn't know that this is all about envy. As though I didn't know whose tricks these are. They're the tricks of the Head of Department. He did, after all, vow me undying hatred – and so he keeps on attacking me every step of the way. However, let's have a look at another letter. The matter will perhaps explain itself.

Ma chère, Fidèle, *forgive me for not writing for so long. I've been in complete rapture. How right that writer was*

who said that love is a second life. Besides, there are now
great changes taking place at home. The Kammerjunker
visits us every day. Sophie is madly in love with him. Papa
is very jolly. I've even heard from our Gregory, who sweeps
floors and talks to himself most of the time, that there'll
soon be a wedding, because Papa *definitely wants to see*
Sophie married to a general or a Kammerjunker *or an*
army colonel…

What the devil! I can't read on… It's all *Kammerjunkers* or
generals. All that's best in this world goes to *Kammerjunkers*
or generals. You find yourself some modest treasure, you think
you'll be able to get hold of it – a *Kammerjunker* or a general
snatches it away from you. To hell with it! I'd want to become
a general myself, not only to win her hand and the rest – no,
I'd want to be a general to see how they'd grovel and use all
their courtly ways and double entendres, and then I'd say to
them that I spat on you both. To hell with it! How frustrating!
I've torn that stupid little dog's letter to bits.

3rd December

It can't be. It's all lies! There's to be no wedding! So what if he's
a *Kammerjunker*. After all it's nothing more than a form of
distinction, not some visible thing you can hold in your hand.
After all the fact that you're a *Kammerjunker* doesn't give you

a third eye on your forehead. After all his nose isn't made of gold; it's just a nose like mine or anyone else's: he uses it to smell and not to eat with, to sneeze and not to cough. There have been a few times when I've wanted to figure out why there are all these distinctions. What makes me a titular councillor and for what reason am I a titular councillor? Could I perhaps be some count or general and only appear to be a titular councillor? Perhaps I don't know myself who I am. There are plenty of examples in history after all: take some simple fellow – not a nobleman – just a simple petty bourgeois or even a peasant – and it's suddenly revealed that he's some grandee or even a sovereign. If that can happen to some muzhik, then what could result from a member of the nobility? For example, if all of a sudden I appear in a general's uniform: I have an epaulette on my right shoulder and an epaulette on my left shoulder and a blue ribbon across the shoulder – what then? How will my beauty sing then? What would her *papa*, our director, say then? Oh, he's a very ambitious man! He's a freemason, definitely a freemason, although he pretends to be this and that, but I instantly noticed that he was a freemason: when he gives someone a hand he only sticks out two fingers. So couldn't I this very minute be appointed governor general or quartermaster or something or other? I'd like to know what makes me a titular councillor? Why precisely a titular councillor?

I spent all morning reading the newspapers. There are strange goings-on in Spain.* I couldn't quite make them out. They write that the throne has been left vacant and that the nobles are in a tricky position when it comes to choosing a successor, which is why there are riots. I think this is extremely odd. How can the throne be left vacant? They say that some *doña* should ascend the throne. A *doña* can't ascend the throne. She really can't. On the throne there has to be a king. They do say that there's no king, but it can't be that there's no king. A country can't exist without a king. There is a king, but he's somewhere out of sight. It may be that he's elsewhere for some family reasons or he's in danger from neighbouring powers: from France or other countries that have forced him into hiding, or perhaps there are other reasons.

8th December

I had every intention of going to the office, but various reasons and preoccupations held me back. I just couldn't get what's happening in Spain out of my head. How can a *doña* become queen? They won't allow such a thing. And first of all, England won't allow it. And besides, those are political matters for the whole of Europe: the Austrian emperor, our sovereign... I confess that I have felt so devastated and stunned by these events that I absolutely couldn't engage in anything all day. Mavra remarked that I'd been terribly distracted at dinner.

And indeed it appears that I absent-mindedly threw two plates to the floor and that they were instantly smashed to pieces. After dinner I walked round the ice slides.* I couldn't derive anything edifying from that. I lay most of the time on my bed going over the Spanish events.

Year 2000, 43rd April

Today is a day of huge celebrations! In Spain there is a king. He has turned up. That king is me. I've only just found out about it today. I confess that it was as if I'd suddenly been struck by lightning. I don't understand how I could have thought and imagined myself to be a titular councillor. When did such a crazy notion enter my head? It's as well that no one thought of putting me in a lunatic asylum. Everything has now opened up before me. I can now see everything as on the palm of my hand. And I don't understand what went on before. Everything ahead seemed cloaked in some kind of fog. And this all happens, I think, because people imagine that the human brain is situated in the head. That's absolutely not so: it gets carried by the wind from the direction of the Caspian Sea. To begin with, I announced to Mavra who I was. When she heard that the King of Spain was standing before her, she wrung her hands and almost died of fright. The stupid woman had never seen the King of Spain before. I, however, tried to calm her down and with kindly words tried to convince her of my goodwill and that I wasn't angry at all for the fact that she had some-times given my boots a bad clean. She's just of peasant stock after all. You can't speak to those people of higher things. She was frightened, because she firmly believed that all the kings of Spain were like Philip II. But I explained to her that there was no similarity at all between myself and Philip, and that I didn't have a single Capuchin friar with me*... I didn't go to the office...To hell with it! No, my friends, you won't entice me there now; I'll no longer copy your vile documents!

86th Marchtober. Between day and night
Today our administrator came round to order me to go to the office, since it's already over three weeks that I haven't been to work. I went to the office for a laugh. The Head of Department thought that I would bow to him and start apologizing, but I just stared at him with indifference, neither too angrily nor too favourably, and I sat down as though unaware of anyone being there. I looked at all that office riff-raff and thought: "If you only knew who's sitting amongst you... My God! What a fuss you'd make, and even the Department Head himself would begin to bow right down to the ground, as he now does to the Director." They placed some documents for me to summarize in front of me. Yet I didn't lift a finger. A few moments later there was a sudden flurry. They said that the Director was on his way. Several officials rushed forward, vying with each other

to be seen by him. But I didn't move an inch. When he walked round our department, they all buttoned up their coats, but I didn't do a thing! What kind of director was he that I should get up before him – never! A director, him? He's just a cork, not a director. An ordinary cork, a simple cork, nothing more. Of the kind they cork bottles with. I found it even more amusing when they slipped me a document to sign. They thought that I would write at the very bottom of the sheet: desk head such and such. Nothing of the kind! In the most important place, where the Director of the Department usually signs, I scribbled: Ferdinand VIII. The reverential silence that ensued was a sight to behold, but I only gestured with my hand saying: "There's no need at all for tokens of servility!" And with that I left the room. From there I made my way straight to the Director's apartment. He wasn't in. The footman didn't want to let me in, but I said something to him which made him drop his arms. I went straight to the boudoir. She had been sitting in front of the mirror, and jumped up and backed away from me. However, I didn't tell her that I was the King of Spain. I only told her that happiness such as she couldn't even imagine was in store for her and that, despite the machinations of the enemy, we'd be together. I didn't want to add anything else and left the room. Oh, what cunning creatures they are – women! Only now have I grasped what a woman really is. No one knew until now who she's in love with: I've been the first to discover it. Woman is in love with the Devil. I'm not joking. Physicists have written nonsense – that she is like this or that – all she loves is the Devil. See for yourselves, she's peering through her lorgnette from the theatre box in the first circle. You think she's looking at that fat man wearing a medal? Not at all: she's looking at the Devil who's behind his back. Look, he's now hiding inside that medal. See, he's beckoning at her with his finger! And she'll marry him. She will. And all their high-ranking fathers, who wriggle their way in everywhere and climb their way to court and call themselves patriots, they're all after rental payments,* these patriots! They'd sell their mother, father, God for money, those ambitious people, those Judases! All this ambition is because they've got a small blister under the tongue with a tiny worm no bigger than a pinhead in it, and it's all the work of some barber who lives in Gorokhaya Street. I don't remember his name, but it's a well-known fact that, together with some midwife, he wants to spread Muhammadanism throughout the world, and they say that as a result already a large section of the population in France has accepted the faith of Muhammad.

No date at all – the day had no date

I walked incognito along Nevsky Prospect. Our Sovereign the Emperor drove past. Everyone in town removed his hat, as did I – I didn't, however, betray the fact that I was the King of Spain. I considered it unseemly to reveal myself in front of everyone, because first of all I have to present myself at court. I've only been held back so far by the fact that I don't have a king's attire. Could I but get hold of some kind of mantle. I would have ordered one from a tailor, but they're complete asses and, besides, they pay little attention to their work, have got caught up in speculation and mostly spend their time paving the streets. I resolved to have a mantle made from my new uniform, which I'd worn only twice. But to avoid those scoundrels making a hash of it, I've decided to sew it myself, after locking the door so that no one could see me. I've cut the whole of it up with a pair of scissors, because it has to be in a completely different style.

The date I don't remember. Nor was there a month. The Devil knows what it was

The mantle is quite ready now. Mavra shrieked when I put it on. However, I still can't make up my mind to present myself at court. There's so far been no delegation from Spain. It's not suitable without delegates. My dignity would lack weight. I expect them any moment now.

The 1st

I'm extremely surprised by the delegates' slow progress. What reasons could be holding them up? Could it be France? Yes, it's the most unfavourably disposed power. I went to check at the post office whether any Spanish delegates had arrived. But the postmaster is particularly stupid and doesn't know a thing: no, he says, there are no Spanish delegates here, but if you wish to write some letters we'll accept them at the established rate. What the Devil! What's a letter? A letter is just drivel. Chemists write letters…

Madrid. Februarius thirtieth

So I'm in Spain and it's all happened so quickly that I've hardly been able to recover my senses. This morning the Spanish delegates appeared and I went off with them in a carriage. The unusual speed at which we went seemed odd to me. We drove so fast that we reached the Spanish border within half an hour. But then there are railway lines across the whole of Europe these days, and ships sail extremely fast. What a strange country Spain is: when we came into the first room I saw a great number of people with shaven heads. I guessed, however, that they had to be grandees or soldiers, because they shave their heads. The Chancellor of State's behaviour seemed to me altogether strange as he led me by the arm. He pushed me into a small room and said: "Sit down, and if you're going to call yourself King Ferdinand I'll beat that urge out of you." But knowing that this was no other than temptation, I replied in the negative, and the Chancellor hit me with a stick twice on the back so painfully that I almost cried out, but checked myself, remembering that this was a chivalric custom when acceding to a higher rank, because to this day they follow the code of chivalry in Spain. Left on my own I decided to occupy myself with government business. I discovered that China and Spain are absolutely one and the same country, and that only out of ignorance are they considered separate nations. I advise everyone to write down carefully the word Spain on a piece of paper, and the word China will appear. I was, however, particularly distressed to learn about the event that is to take place tomorrow. Tomorrow at seven o'clock there is to be a strange phenomenon: the earth will land on the moon. The famous English chemist Wellington writes about this. I confess that I felt uneasy in my heart when I imagined the moon's singular tenderness and fragility. The moon is usually made in Hamburg, you see, and it's very badly made too. I'm amazed that England isn't turning its attention to that. A lame cooper makes it, and it's obvious that the fool has no understanding of the moon at all. He's put together some tarred rope and low-grade lamp oil, which is why there's a horrible smell all over our earth that makes you hold your nose. That's why the moon herself is such a tender ball that people can't live there at all and only noses live there. And that's why we can't see our own noses at all, as they're all on the moon. So when I imagined our earth to be of heavy substance and that when landing it could grind our noses to flour, I was overcome by such uneasiness that, having put on my stockings and shoes, I hurried to the State Council Hall to order the police not to allow the earth to land on the moon. The shaven grandees, a great many of whom I found in the State Council Hall, were very intelligent people, and when I said "Gentlemen, let's save the moon, because the earth wants to land on her", they all immediately rushed off to fulfil my royal wish, and many clambered up the walls to get hold of the moon – but at that moment the Great Chancellor came in, and when they saw him they all scattered. I, as King, remained on my own. But the Chancellor, to my amazement, hit me with the stick and banished me to my room. Such is the power of national customs in Spain!

January of that same year, which fell after February

I still fail to understand what kind of a land Spain is. Their customs and court etiquette are completely unusual. I don't understand, I don't understand, I really don't understand a thing. Today they shaved my head, although I screamed with all my might that I didn't want to be a monk. But I can't even remember what took hold of me when they began to trickle cold water down my head. I've never been through such hellish torment before. I was about to fly into a rage, and they were hardly able to hold me back. I don't understand the meaning of that strange custom at all. It's a stupid, senseless custom! The recklessness of those kings who have still not abolished it defeats me. Judging by all probabilities I now suspect that I may have fallen into the hands of the Inquisition, and that the one I took to be the Chancellor of State is the Grand Inquisitor himself. But I still can't understand how a king can be subjected to the Inquisition. It could, in truth, be orchestrated by France – and by Polignac* in particular, Oh, what a rogue that Polignac is! He's sworn to persecute me to death. And so he goes on pursuing me, but I know, my friend, that you're led by the English. The Englishman is a great politician. He wriggles his way into everything. It's common knowledge that when England takes snuff, France sneezes.

The 25th

Today the Grand Inquisitor came into my room, but having heard his footsteps from afar I hid under the chair. When he couldn't see me, he began to call me. At first he shouted: "Poprishchin!" – and not a word from me. Then: "Aksenty Ivanov! Titular Councillor! Nobleman!' And I still kept silent. "Ferdinand VIII, King of Spain!" I wanted to poke my head out, but then thought: "No, brother, you won't fool me! We know you: you'll trickle more cold water over my head." He caught sight of me, however, and drove me from under the chair with his stick. That damned stick really hurts. Nevertheless I was rewarded for all this by today's revelation: I found out that every cock has its Spain hidden under its feathers. The Grand

Inquisitor, however, angrily left the room, threatening me with some punishment or other. But I was totally scornful of his impotent anger, as I knew that he was acting like a machine, the Englishman's tool.

Da 34, te, Mth yare, ɅɹɐnɹqǝℲ 349

No, I can't take any more. My God! What are they doing to me! They're pouring cold water over my head! They're not hearing, seeing me or listening to me. What have I done to them? Why are they torturing me? What do they want from me, poor me? What can I give them? I don't have anything. I haven't got the strength, I can't bear this torment, my head is burning and everything is spinning round before me. Save me! Take me away! Give me a troika with horses of whirlwind speed! Sit down, my driver, ring out, my bells, fly up, horses, and carry me away from this world! Farther and farther, so that nothing more can be seen, nothing. There, the sky is swirling before me; a little star twinkles in the distance; the forest rushes on with its dark trees and the moon; a blue-grey mist spreads out under my feet; a string twangs in the mist; there's the sea on one side and, on the other... Italy; and now Russian log huts come to view. Is that my house showing blue in the distance? Is that my mother sitting by the window? Mother, save your poor son! Drop a tear on his aching little head! Watch how they're tormenting me! Hold your poor little orphan to your bosom! There's nowhere for him on earth! They're driving him away! Mother, have pity on your sick little child! And did you know that the Dey* of Algeria has a lump right under his nose?

Note on the Text

The translations of 'Nevsky Prospect', 'The Nose' and 'The Overcoat' are based on the texts from Nikolai Gogol, *Peterburgskie Povesti* (Moscow: Izdatel'stvo, "Kudozhestvennaya Literatura", 1965). The translation of 'Diary of a Madman' is based on the text from Nikolai Gogol, *Povesti* (Moscow: Eksmo, "Russkaya klassika", 2012).

Notes

p. 3, *Nevsky Prospect*: Nevsky Prospect (or Avenue) is the main street in St Petersburg, which runs from the Admiralty to the Alexander Nevsky Monastery. Today it still functions as the city's main thoroughfare.

p. 4, *the Petersburg or Vyborg... Peski or the Moscow Gate*: The centre of St Petersburg is on the left bank of the River Neva; the Petersburg district is situated between the Little Neva and the Nevka, two branches of the River Neva. The Vyborg district, Peski and the Moscow Gate are other areas, which in Gogol's time were remote from each other.

p. 5, *Ganymede*: A handsome Trojan youth in Greek mythology, who was a cup-bearer to the gods.

p. 5, *the Catherine Canal*: The Catherine Canal had sewage flowing into it, hence Gogol's sarcastic remark about its purity. In 1923 it was renamed Griboyedov Canal, after the writer Alexander Griboyedov (1795–1829).

p. 5, *grivna*: Obsolete unit of currency worth ten copecks.

p. 6, *the blessed title of officials with special responsibilities*: During his reign Peter the Great introduced what is known as the Table of Ranks (1722), a formal list of the positions and ranks in the civil service, the military and the court. There were fourteen ranks which determined the position and status of everybody according to service. This eventually had the effect of creating an educated class of noble bureaucrats. A civil servant promoted to the fourteenth grade was endowed with personal nobility, and anyone above the ninth rank gained the status of hereditary nobility. The Table of Ranks went as follows:

Civil Service	Military	Court
1) Chancellor	General Field Marshal/Admiral	
2) Actual Privy Councillor	General	Chief Chamberlain
3) Privy Councillor	Lieutenant General	Marshal of the House
4) Actual State Councillor	Major General	Chamberlain
5) State Councillor	Brigadier	Master of Ceremonies
6) Collegiate Councillor	Colonel	Chamber Fourrier
7) Court Councillor	Lieutenant Colonel	

8) Collegiate Assessor	Major	House Fourrier
9) Titular Councillor	Staff-Captain	
10) Collegiate Secretary	Lieutenant	
11) Ship Secretary	*Kammerjunker*	
12) Government Secretary	Sub-Lieutenant	
13) Provincial Secretary		
14) Collegiate Registrar	Senior Ensign	

p. 8, A*dmiralty Spire*: The golden spire of Admiralty building, a famous St Petersburg landmark, visible from Nevsky Prospect.

p. 12, *Perugino's Bianca*: A picture of the Madonna in the fresco *The Adoration of the Magi* painted by Pietro Vannucci (1446–1523), otherwise known as Perugino. It is named after the chapel of Santa Maria de' Bianchi in Città della Pieve.

p. 25, *Kammerjunkers*: Literally, "a gentleman of the bedchamber" (German), one of the lowest courtier ranks.

p. 39, *Bulgarin, Pushkin and Grech... A.A. Orlov*: F.V. Bulgarin (1789–1859) and N.I. Grech (1787–1867) were minor writers and journalists, editors of *The Northern Bee*, a very popular privately owned reactionary newspaper published in St Petersburg. They appealed to the social group that Pirogov belonged to, which was loyal to the government. Here they are mentioned in the same breath as the great poet Alexander Pushkin, who used to mock them, and it is

Gogol's way of ridiculing their undiscriminating knowledge of literature. A.A. Orlov (1791–1840) was another minor author.

p. 39, *Filatkas*: A reference to popular vaudevilles *Filatka and Miroshka* and *Filatka and Her Children* by P.I. Grigoryev (1807–54).

p. 40, *Dmitry Donskoy and Woe from Wit*: *Dmitry Donskoy* by V.A. Ozerov (1769–1816) and *Woe from Wit* by A.S. Griboyedov (1795–1829) are plays in verse. *Woe from Wit* has remained a famous classic play to this day.

p. 40, *the anecdote about the cannon ... being another*: An anecdote about the Empress Catherine II asking some general what the difference was between a cannon and a unicorn, to which the general replied that the cannon was one thing and the unicorn another. The Empress is alleged to have replied: "Oh now I understand." In fact a unicorn was a cannon with the engraving of a unicorn on it. Prince P.A. Vyazemsky (1792–1878) tells this story in his *Old Notebook*.

p. 43, *rapé:* A superior type of snuff.

p. 46, *Meine Frau!*: "My wife!" (German).

p. 46, *Was wollen Sie doch?*: "What do you want?" (German).

p. 46, *"Gehen Sie*: "Go" (German).

p. 53, *The Northern Bee*: See first note to p. 39.

p. 57, *Collegiate Assessor Kovalyov*: See note to p. 6.

p. 62, *those collegiate assessors... in the Caucasus*: It was much easier to attain this rank in the Caucasus than in St Petersburg, and the usual examination required could be bypassed there.

p. 62, *Major*: This was the military rank equivalent to collegiate assessor in the civil service, but military ranks were regarded as more prestigious.

p. 75, *The Northern Bee*: See first note to p. 39.

p. 76, that nasty Berezinsky snuff: Poor-quality local tobacco.

p. 88, *Junker's Store:* A fashionable shop not far from Nevsky Prospect.

p. 89, *Tauride Garden*: A popular garden to this day, the Tauride Garden was laid out in 1783–89 on the estate of Grigory Potemkin, behind the Tauride Palace in St Petersburg.

p. 89, *Khozrev-Mirza*: Persian prince who came to Russia in 1829 to apologize for the murder in Tehran of the poet and playwright Alexander Griboyedov (1795–1829). He stayed in the Tauride Palace.

p. 90, *trepak*: Lively Ukrainian folk dance.

p. 93, *Gostiny Dvor:* On Nevsky Prospect; it is not only the city's oldest and largest shopping centre, but also one of the first shopping arcades in the world.

p. 97, *Khozdazat*: A fourth-century lawyer who converted to Christianity and became a bishop.

p. 97, *calendar*: The Russian Orthodox calendar, which lists saints' days and feast days.

p. 103, *Falconet's horse*: This refers to the statue of Peter the Great in St Petersburg by the French sculptor Étienne Maurice Falconet (1716–91). He is represented on a horse rearing on its hind legs, and the third point of support is his tail – which, if cut, would mean the collapse of the statue.

p. 134, *given an official seal*: It was customary to seal off with an official seal the premises and belongings of anyone who died without heirs until arrangements were made for their disposal.

p. 143, *sharpen His Excellency's quills*: It was the duty of minor clerks to sharpen their superiors' quills and it was sometimes a means of furthering their careers.

p. 144, *nobility*: See note to p. 6. References to the nobility indicate that the narrator Poprishchin is on Rank 12 or above on the Table of Ranks.

p. 147, *Zverkov's house*: The first five-storey building in St Petersburg, on the Ekaterininsky Canal. Gogol lived there between 1829 and 1831.

p. 148, *Little Bee*: I.e. *The Northern Bee*; see first note to p. 39.

p. 148, *those French*: A reference to the 1830 revolution and what followed.

p. 148, *Kursk*: An ancient town about six hundred miles from St Petersburg.

p. 149, *Pushkin's verse*: Certainly not by Pushkin, these verses are a parody of some verses by N.P. Nikolev (1758–1815), a minor poet and playwright.

p. 151, *Ruch's tailcoat*: Ruch was a fashionable tailor in St Petersburg at the time.

p. 151, *Filatka*: See second note to p. 39.

p. 160, *Kammerjunker*: See note to p. 25.

p. 165, *strange goings-on in Spain*: A reference to the civil unrest on the death of Ferdinand VII (1784–1833) in 1833. It became a power struggle between those who wanted Ferdinand's brother Don Carlos (1788–1855) on the throne and the supporters of his three-year-old daughter Isabella, who did in fact succeed to the throne. These events were certainly reported in the *Northern Bee*, avidly read by Poprishchin.

p. 166, *ice slides*: Taking advantage of the long Russian winters, tall wooden ice-glazed structures were set up, nicknamed "the Russian Mountains" and selling thrill rides.

p. 167, *Philip II... a single Capuchin friar with me*: Philip II (1527–98) had a reputation for being cruel. During his reign the Inquisition reached new heights. The Capuchin friars were a newly established order at the time.

p. 169, *rental payments*: A monthly rental income, decreed by the Tsar and paid to senior civil servants for their service.

p. 174, *Polignac*: Prince Jules Armand Marie de Polignac (1780–1847) was an ultra-royalist politician who served as Prime Minister under Charles X, just before the 1830 July Revolution.

p. 176, *Dey*: Title given to the rulers of the Regency of Algiers and Tripoli under the Ottoman Empire from 1671 onwards. The title was no longer used after the conquest of Algeria in 1830, the last Dey being Hussein Pasha (1765–1838).

Acknowledgements

I would like to mention several people who helped and supported me as I was translating the *Petersburg Tales*: Vera Liber for her expert suggestions, Marianna Colyer for her invaluable feedback and encouragement, Dr Janet Sturgis for reading closely through all four tales and Anthony Bales for yet again giving me his time and unswerving support. Thank you all so much!

— Dora O'Brien

Dora O'Brien read Russian and Italian at Victoria University, Wellington, New Zealand, followed by an MA in Russian Language and Literature at SSEES, UCL. She taught in a Moscow state school for a year in the late 1990s and is the author of the memoir *From Moscow* (Bramcote Press, 2000). Her recent translations include *Childhood, Boyhood, Youth* by Leo Tolstoy, *Rudin* by Ivan Turgenev (both Alma Classics) and *Still Water* by Olga Rimsha (Glas).

ALMA CLASSICS

ALMA CLASSICS aims to publish mainstream and lesser-known European classics in an innovative and striking way, while employing the highest editorial and production standards. By way of a unique approach the range offers much more, both visually and textually, than readers have come to expect from contemporary classics publishing.

LATEST TITLES PUBLISHED BY ALMA CLASSICS

209   Giuseppe T. di Lampedusa, *Childhood Memories and Other Stories*
210   Mark Twain, *Is Shakespeare Dead?*
211   Xavier de Maistre, *Journey around My Room*
212   Émile Zola, *The Dream*
213   Ivan Turgenev, *Smoke*
214   Marcel Proust, *Pleasures and Days*
215   Anatole France, *The Gods Want Blood*
216   F. Scott Fitzgerald, *The Last Tycoon*
217   Gustave Flaubert, *Memoirs of a Madman* and *November*
218   Edmondo De Amicis, *Memories of London*
219   E.T.A. Hoffmann, *The Sandman*
220   Sándor Márai, *The Withering World*
221   François Villon, *The Testament and Other Poems*
222   Arthur Conan Doyle, *Tales of Twilight and the Unseen*
223   Robert Musil, *The Confusions of Young Master Törless*
224   Nikolai Gogol, *Petersburg Tales*
225   Franz Kafka, *The Metamorphosis and Other Stories*
226   George R. Sims, *Memoirs of a Mother-in-Law*
227   Virginia Woolf, *Monday or Tuesday*
228   F. Scott Fitzgerald, *Basil and Josephine*
229. F. Scott Fitzgerald, *Flappers and Philosophers*
230   Dante Alighieri, *Love Poems*
231   Charles Dickens, *The Mudfog Papers*
232   Dmitry Merezhkovsky, *Leonardo da Vinci*
233   Ivan Goncharov, *Oblomov*
234   Alexander Pushkin, *Belkin's Stories*
235   Mikhail Bulgakov, *Black Snow*

To order any of our titles and for up-to-date information about our current and forthcoming publications, please visit our website on:

www.almaclassics.com